THE SAM HOLLI

Dying to Write

Is a story worth dying for?

Honor Brightwell

Paperback ISBN: 978-1-0684791-2-0

eBook ISBN: 978-1-0684791-3-7

Published in the United Kingdom by Honor Brightwell.

Printed by Amazon.

Cover design by BespokeAuthor.com

For my favourite story writers:
Niamh and Isla

February 2024

'She said *what?'* He half rose from his chair, hands pushing against the edge of the table, chin jutting, scowl in place.

'You heard,' she said, turning away to stir the pan on the stove, letting his initial flare of anger subside. 'A book, she said. The friend she stayed here with has written a book based on Alwyn Hall. And she did the illustrations for it. It's going to be published soon.'

'Since when do you have time for all this chit-chat? I've told you before, don't get pulled into conversation.'

'She was just chatting. I think she thought we'd want to buy a few copies.'

'What's her name?'

'Can't remember. Something short—Jess, Jane? Her friend stayed here before, with a school trip. Adam something?'

He pulled a scuffed, A4 notebook towards him. Licking one of his fingers, oblivious to the grime, he turned the pages to find the booking. His finger left a faint trail on the page.

'Got them. Jen Somerville and Aidan Wilcox. Google them, see if you can find out anything about this book.'

Her eyebrows twitched in protest of the order. 'No. You do it. I've got work to do.'

Grabbing her shoulder as she turned away he replied. 'And you think I haven't? Is that it? If we don't shut this book down right now we're in deep shit.'

'You will be. Not me.'

'You stupid woman, you're an accessory.'

'You've been watching too many crime dramas.'

'And maybe yours will be the next body.'

She shrugged her shoulder away, sniffed, and returned to stirring the pan, ignoring the slamming of the outer door and his retreating footsteps.

March 2024

It was unusual for Aidan to receive a letter, especially one that arrived in a handwritten envelope. But there it was, quietly waiting its turn for attention amidst the luridly bright flyers advertising take-away pizzas and curries. The flyers went in the bin, the letter on to the kitchen worktop. An unassuming sort of envelope, but even so, Aidan wasn't entirely sure he wanted to open it. Why would someone take the time to send an old-fashioned letter? Why not call, or send a message? Did it bring good news or bad?

He picked up the envelope and scrutinised it for clues about the sender. The address was written in capitals. The jauntily-angled stamp was smeared with the postmark which was unreadable. He sighed, filled the kettle to make coffee, and perched on the breakfast bar stool, feet easily reaching the kitchen floor.

Coffee made, he prised open the stuck-down flap and took out a single sheet of cheap, folded paper. It looked as though it had been torn from an A4 notepad, with two holes handily punched for filing, and lined to encourage neat writing. But the writer of this letter hadn't *written* on the paper. They had cut the words they wanted from a book or magazine, and stuck them on the page. Untidy it may be, but the message was clear:

Kill the book or we kill you

Aidan blinked and read it again. Surely it was only in murder mysteries that people sent letters like this. Miss Marple would be knocking on the door next. Clichéd for sure, but it was unsettling, becoming more so every time he read it. He scrunched the paper up into a ball and hurled it into the rubbish bin. Turning the tap on full, he pumped the plunger of the soap bottle vigorously until his hands were slimy with liquid soap. Rubbing his skin until it felt tender and raw, he still couldn't quite rid himself of feeling—what was the word? Yes, that was it: *contaminated.*

His mind kept playing the single line of the letter. *Kill the book or we kill you.* That could only mean his book. The one he'd recently finished writing. The one Phoenix Publishing wanted to launch for the Christmas market. The one currently on his laptop: the story that had evolved into a graphic novel with, in his opinion, the most striking illustrations he'd ever seen. A click of the delete button would make it all disappear. But he'd spent months on it. And months working with the illustrator. Why should he kill it on the orders of someone who hid behind an anonymous letter? What was the saying? *Publish and be damned,* he thought. *Hope it won't end up being publish and die.*

The shrilling of the alarm made Aidan jump. A restless night, spent thinking about the letter and about his book. He sighed. His mind kept going back to where the idea for the story had started. Alwyn Hall. His school had booked it for the Year 6 residential trip. The trip nearly hadn't happened as someone forgot to book the accommodation, and Alwyn Hall was the only place available at short notice. Just the name Alwyn Hall conjured up the feeling of unease that had kicked in from the moment the front door opened.

January 2023

The chatter reached a sudden crescendo as one of the children shouted above the hubbub 'We're here! I saw the sign!'

'Let's get off this coach before I puke,' said one pale-looking boy.

'Urgh, not over me,' shrieked the girl sitting next to him. A chant of 'Freddie's throwing up, Freddie's throwing up' started, with the rest of the school children soon joining in, and only stopping as the coach turned in to a driveway and drew to a halt. The grey-stoned building in front of them had obviously been rather grand in its day. Despite its shabby exterior, with chipped white paintwork on the windows and doors, Alwyn Hall managed to convey its disapproval of the watery sunshine that tried to brighten it.

'Is this it, Mr Wilcox?' asked one of the children. 'Bit posh. It's got three floors! And a tower!' The children crowded to the side of the coach closest to Alwyn Hall.

'Looks a bit creepy to me,' said one of the boys. 'Bet it's haunted.'

'Yeah, the ghost'll be up in that tower. Can we sleep up there, Mr Wilcox?' asked another.

Ignoring the children's first impressions, Aidan started to

organise the transfer of thirty children from the coach to the Hall. 'The sign says 'Alwyn Hall' so yes, we're here. No, back in your seats,' said Aidan as the children made to stampede off the coach. 'Let's get off row by row, starting with the front.'

There was a groan, but the children sat back down, perching on their seats, wielding their backpacks like shields, as Aidan made his way to the front of the coach to supervise their arrival.

Eventually, the last child left the coach, and bags were off-loaded and reunited with their owners on the gravel path outside the front door which remained firmly closed. The sash windows either side of the door looked out blankly, giving no hint of anyone inside the building.

Aidan went up to the door with its faded paintwork, and pushed it. 'It's locked,' he said, looking for a bell. 'Oh here, let's try this.' There was a loud ringing. 'At least we know the bell works,' he said brightly to the group of impatiently waiting children.

The door opened reluctantly to reveal a man in his fifties. His thinning grey hair was pulled back into a ponytail. His glasses slid down his nose, and with a sniff, he pushed them back into place, peering uncertainly at Aidan. 'Oh,' he said. 'It's you. Hello.'

'Er, hello. I'm Aidan Wilcox, one of the teachers from West Langley Primary School,' said Aidan smiling as he extended his hand.

'Rodric Morgan, general dogsbody,' replied the man, pulling his lips back into a grin that showed his discoloured teeth. 'Call me Morgan. Everyone does.' *A smoker* thought Aidan, as he shook hands.

'So,' said Morgan, casting his eye over the group of children. 'This is the rabble then,' grinning to soften his words. 'You'd better come inside. You'll want to get them settled in. When are you going back?'

'Er, Friday. We've booked for four nights for four teachers and thirty children,' said Aidan.

'Yeah, you're booked. You've got two floors—first and second. Girls on the first, boys on the second. Food's served in the dining room on the ground floor. There's a room next to it where you pick up your outdoor gear. I'll be in there from eight tomorrow morning. No poking around the rest of the building, or outside: it's out of bounds. There's a lot of maintenance work going on.'

'What about the zip line? I read there's an outdoor area for the kids to play in.'

'Not this week,' said Morgan. 'Not safe. The ropes have been taken down until it can be checked and repaired. Don't want any accidents, do we.'

'No … no, of course not,' said Aidan, feeling disappointed for the children. 'Right then, we'll get our stuff in and get sorted out.'

'You'll find drinks and snacks in the dining room if the kids want something before supper. You need to supervise them though. Meal times are on the board in the dining room.'

Aidan turned to the children and said 'OK, listen up. Girls are on the first floor. Go up now with Miss Mills and Mrs Spires. Boys, and Mr Davies, we're on the second floor. Get your things sorted, your beds made up, and we'll meet in the dining room on the ground floor at 4pm. Don't go wandering off to other parts of the house, or outside: it's out of bounds to us because there's maintenance work going on. Everyone know what they're doing?'

There were nods and 'yes, Mr Wilcox' as the children started to go inside, trailing their bags behind them. Aidan waited until the last child was indoors, and spoke to the coach driver before starting to head up to the second floor. Above him, thirty pairs of feet clomped noisily on the bare, wooden stairs.

'Oh, what's the drill if a teacher needs to speak to one of the hostel staff?' asked Aidan, turning back to see Morgan locking the front door.

'Ring the bell. The buzzer's right here,' he said, pointing to a button on the wall by the stairs. 'There's only me and the kitchen staff here at this time of the year. You're the only group booked for this week. Keep the kids under control. We wouldn't want to see them sent home for unruly behaviour.' He grinned again, before walking along the corridor and unlocking another door marked private.

Oh, I bet you would, thought Aidan as he continued up the stairs. *You're polite enough, but I feel about as welcome as a hailstorm in July.*

The room didn't invite Aidan to make himself at home. The best part of it wasn't the décor, but the view through the small, sashed window. Despite the grime on the glass, Aidan could just make out the hills beyond, the last of the winter light highlighting the contours of the slopes.

The bedside table was just big enough for his washbag, and there was a hook on the back of the door for either a coat or a towel. He tried pulling out a drawer from the chest of drawers, but it didn't run freely and made the whole unit wobble. He decided to leave his clothes in his bag. *It's not as if I've brought my dinner jacket,* he thought to himself. He tried the bed. *Not bad,* he thought.

He knocked on the door of his co-teacher, Gavin Davies. Gavin's room was the same as Aidan's.

'Cheerful place, isn't it,' grinned Gavin, smoothing his beard into shape. 'I gave up on unpacking.'

'Yeah, my stuff's staying in my bag too. It'll feel livelier once our lot get settled in, although I've already been warned that unruly children will be sent home,' said Aidan. 'Let's round them up and get off to the dining room. Maybe we can rustle up some hot drinks and biscuits.'

'I'm sure our charming host is putting out the jammie dodgers even as we speak,' said Gavin.

'Now you're talking! Jammie dodgers …' replied Aidan as he left the room, calling in briefly to each of the small dormitories where the boys would be sleeping. The rooms were even more basic than his bedroom, with bunk beds and a cupboard alongside each bunk.

'OK kids,' he called, 'everyone downstairs.'

'Did you say there'd be jammie dodgers, Mr Wilcox?' asked Freddie.

'If you're extremely lucky,' said Aidan. A cheer went up, as the children jostled with one another to go back down the stairs.

'You sound like a herd of elephants!' said Aidan, wincing at the sound of clattering feet on bare boards.

'Can't help it. No carpet. It's a bit—well, basic, isn't it,' commented Noah, one of the group.

'It's got all we need: beds, meals, showers,' said Aidan.

'Showers? We don't need showers! I only had one last night,' said Charlie, looking horrified.

'Nah, don't need 'em,' agreed Noah.

'We do need biscuits though,' said Freddie, looking worried.

'All you think about is food,' said Charlie, grinning at Freddie.

'Well, it's important!' said Freddie. 'Isn't it, Mr Wilcox?'

'It is. So let's get down to the dining room and see what's on offer,' replied Aidan.

'Come on, kids, as quickly but as quietly as you can, please,' added Gavin.

Turning at the foot of the stairs, Gavin took the only way that looked open to them: a long corridor, with mustard-yellow walls, stretched ahead. Doors, painted dark brown, led off the corridor and had 'private' on them. *They look like dollops of chocolate pudding floating in custard* thought Gavin as he passed door after door with Aidan and the children snaking behind him. Eventually he reached a door with glass panels that opened into a large, high-ceilinged room furnished with long wooden tables and bench seats. At one end, a hatch linked the dining room with the kitchen. In front of it, a table held urns, mugs, and jugs of water. No biscuits.

'Hi there,' called Aidan, putting his head into the hatch. 'Oh, hello,' he said, as a young girl came over to see what he wanted. 'We've just arrived, and the kids are hungry. Any chance of some biscuits?'

The girl looked at him, a slight frown creasing her forehead. 'Please?' she said, in a foreign-sounding voice.

'Biscuits? Could we have some biscuits?' asked Aidan, as he did a quick mime of eating. *She only looks about sixteen. Wonder what she's doing here? Can't be work experience, surely,* he thought.

'Ah,' said the girl, and went back into the kitchen. Opening up a few cupboards, she eventually found some packets and brought them to the hatch. Showing them to Aidan, she looked at him quizzically. He looked at the packets: custard creams, bourbons and yes, jammie dodgers! He smiled, and thanked her. She didn't return his smile, but turned away. *Scuttling away,* thought Aidan. *What's her problem?*

The boys, now sitting at the tables, looked expectantly at the packets in Aidan's hands. 'We'll have to share them with the girls,' he said. A groan went up, and a few half-hearted protestations, just as the girls and their teachers came through the door.

'Oooh, biscuits,' said Mia, coming forward to claim one, with her friends close behind her.

'Yes,' said Aidan. 'Come up a few at a time to get something to drink. We don't want a stampede. There's tea, coffee, water, or squash. I'll put some biscuits on each table for you to share. *Share*, remember,' he said, as hands shot out to claim the best ones.

The hubbub quietened for as long as the biscuits lasted, by which time the teachers were ready to brief them on activities, where to find outdoor coats and boots, and the times for supper and breakfast.

With the children in their beds, full up with biscuits and a surprisingly good supper, the four teachers met in the dining room. The hatch doors that opened to the kitchen were now shut, and the bench tables were laid for breakfast. Without anywhere else to get together, the teachers settled as best they could on the bench seats, hoping to relax with a glass of wine or beer.

'I thought they were never going to settle down. There's still a bit of giggling going on but I think they're all tired,' said Freya, the oldest of the four teachers. In her jeans and fleece, and face devoid of makeup, she looked younger than her forty years.

'Red or white? Or there's beer,' Nadia asked, offering to pour. 'Glad we thought to bring some supplies with us.'

'Red, please,' said Freya. 'Ooh, nice nails. Not sure they'll look like that by the time we go home though.'

'Oh well, it'll be a good excuse to get them done again,' said Nadia, flicking her hair away from her eyes, framed with heavy mascara and perfect eyebrows.

There was a pause while they savoured the first sips of their wine, or for Gavin, a beer.

'What do you make of this place?' asked Gavin, wiping some froth off his beard. 'Bit of an off-hand welcome, I thought.'

'Yes, it was. And the girl in the kitchen didn't seem to understand English,' said Aidan. 'In fact, she looked quite nervous.'

'You probably scared her,' Gavin grinned. 'I'll try her with Welsh tomorrow. We'll get double rations of biscuits for that!'

There was some laughter before Freya commented 'It's a bit—well, a bit closed up. All those locked doors. And the long corridors to get to our rooms, and on this floor too. It all looks so—well, dreary,' said Freya, glancing around. With walls painted in pale grey, wooden floors and basic tables and chairs, it didn't feel welcoming. 'At least there's nothing that the kids can damage,' she added.

'And the lighting's pathetic. I think they must be 40-watt bulbs in our rooms and in the corridors. It's really gloomy, and the décor doesn't do anything for it,' said Nadia, shuddering as she looked around. 'Good thing I brought my mirror with the back light for my room.'

'You're not going to wear make up every day, are you?' asked Freya, her nose wrinkling at the thought of all the effort. 'No one's going to notice if you don't.'

'I won't feel like me if I don't,' said Nadia firmly.

'At least it's warm in the bedrooms,' said Aidan.

'I'm surprised just how warm they are,' said Gavin. 'Almost cosy!'

'I had our Mr Morgan down as a bit of a skinflint,' said Aidan. 'But he's generous with the heating.'

'It's not that warm on our floor,' said Freya. 'Anyway, how did we end up booking this place?'

'It's on the list of approved places that schools can book. There's a budget we have to work with, and this was the only place that could take us for the dates we wanted. I think the booking was made a bit late,' explained Aidan.

'Huh, bet it's a case of book once and never again!' said Nadia, inspecting her nails. The spotted patterning on the black background was really rather pleasing.

'Morgan did say we're the only group booked in for this week.'

'It's not that bad,' said Gavin. Nadia raised her carefully arched eyebrows at him, and he said nothing more.

'Well, I think I'm going to have to head off to get some sleep. It's going to be a long day tomorrow, and goodness knows when the kids will wake up,' said Freya, finishing her wine.

'Good plan. Climbing and abseiling tomorrow for my group. I can't wait!' said Gavin, stretching his neck and shoulders as he got up from the bench.

'Caves and the waterfall walk for mine,' said Nadia, stifling a yawn. 'I suppose there's no shops?'

'Er, it's an outward-bound course?' said Freya. Nadia retreated into the cowl neck of her jumper, and twirled her glass to finish her wine.

'Where do we pick up our gear?' asked Freya.

'The caving and climbing centres supply the equipment. We get waterproofs and boots from the room next to the dining room,' explained Aidan. 'Right, I'll wash up these glasses, you all get off to bed. I'll meet you down here at 7.30. Breakfast is at 8, remember, and we'd better not be late or we'll be in Morgan's bad books,' said Aidan.

'OK, boss,' said Gavin, dodging to avoid the light punch Aidan aimed at his shoulder. 'Only kidding—sir!'

'Twenty-eight, twenty-nine. We're missing somebody,' said Aidan, counting up the children seated around the tables. 'But who is it?' His colleagues had a quick look round.

'Charlie,' said Gavin. 'Where's he got to?' He walked over to the boys who shared a room with Charlie. 'Is Charlie still getting dressed?' he asked.

'Er, don't know,' Noah mumbled. Gavin looked at the boys seated around the table. None of them wanted to meet his eye.

'Come on, is he still upstairs?' Gavin asked.

'Dunno,' said Freddie, shifting uneasily on the wooden bench.

'What's going on? I need to know where he is. We won't be going climbing or abseiling until he's found.'

The boys kept their eyes down, stirring their cereals.

'Mikey, Todd, anything you can tell me?' Gavin asked. 'No one's in trouble. We just need to make sure Charlie is safe.'

Noah fidgeted, and looked up. 'We had this dare,' he started. Mikey and Todd glanced quickly at Noah, before keeping their heads down.

'Go on,' said Gavin.

'We dared him to run round the house and get back in again without being seen,' said Noah. 'We haven't … we haven't seen him since he went off.'

'And when was this?' asked Gavin.

'About half an hour ago,' said Todd. The others nodded in agreement.

Gavin sighed. 'You know everywhere apart from here and our bedrooms are out of bounds? OK, OK, I appreciate you owning up. I'll go and look for him.' Gavin looked up and saw the door to the dining room open.

'One of yours, I believe,' said Morgan, holding the hood of Charlie's sweater to prevent escape. 'Found him lurking around outside. That's out of bounds,' he added.

'I'm sure he's very sorry and he won't do it again, eh, Charlie?' said Gavin.

Charlie looked at his teacher, who gave him a slight nod. 'No, no, I won't. I'm sorry, Mr Morgan.'

'OK?' asked Gavin. Morgan looked from Charlie to Gavin, sighed, and said 'Don't let it happen again. Not any of you.'

'We won't,' said Gavin. 'Now, we need to get our breakfasts so we're ready for the coach. I'll talk to you later, Charlie.'

Two mini buses pulled up outside Alwyn Hall, waiting for the children. The sky was clear, and although there was a chill wind, it was at least dry—for now.

'Everyone got waterproofs and warm clothes with them?' asked Freya. There was a mumbling of agreement.

'Mia's got a pink waterproof,' giggled Olivia.

'Shurrup, you know I hate pink!' said Mia, poking her friend in the ribs.

'As long as it keeps you dry, that's all you need to worry about,' said Freya. 'On the bus now, quickly please.'

'Is it far, miss?' asked Freddie.

'I don't think so.' She scanned down her list quickly. 'Freddie, you're on the other bus with Mr Wilcox and Mrs Spires.'

The children swarmed onto the buses, chattering excitedly.

'Hey, Charlie, did you find anything outside? Can we get up the tower?' called Todd.

'Everything's locked, and the front door locks behind you. That's why I got caught. I couldn't get back in. Mr Morgan saw me and gave me a right telling off,' said Charlie. 'I don't know what his problem is. I was only looking around.'

'Still think it's a bit spooky,' said Noah. 'Anyone hear anything in the night?'

'No, only you snoring,' said Todd. 'You snore like an old man. Ow!' he said, as Charlie landed a punch on his arm.

'Shurrup, you snore too,' said Charlie.

'Don't,' retorted Todd.

'I can see our bedroom window,' said Mikey. 'Look, up there!' The boys craned their necks to see. 'I know it's ours 'cos there's a crack in the bottom pane.'

'Look, the windows above it are all blacked out, like something from the war!' said Todd.

'Probably hasn't been used since World War Two. Or maybe even World War One. What if it was one of those code-breaking places?'

'It's secret enough!' said Charlie.

The bus engine started up, and the boys settled into their seats, anticipating the activities to come.

'Bet I'm the fastest climber,' said Noah.

'Bet I'm the fastest abseiler,' said Charlie.

'Bet Freddie's scared,' said Todd. Freddie scowled, and turned away to look out the window.

Tired children made for a quiet bus. Gavin looked at them, their heads lolling as the bus swayed round the bends of the narrow road. He smiled to himself. A few hours outdoors, learning the basics of climbing and abseiling had worn them out. A few were naturals, others needed more time to practise, and some had to overcome their fear before they could do anything. In the end, everyone had completed at least one ascent and descent.

'I'm proud of them,' he said to Freya. 'They all did well today, in their different ways. Did you enjoy it?'

'I did. I wasn't sure I would, but it was fun. The kids were great. It's good to see how they adapted to an environment they don't know. You've climbed before, haven't you?' said Freya.

'Yes, not exactly Everest, but some low-key stuff. Wonder what's for supper tonight?' said Gavin.

'I'm wondering if we'll get any biscuits when we get in,' said Freya.

'Hungry?' asked Gavin.

'Ravenous. Bet the kids will be too when they wake up.'

The main door was open, and Morgan was standing just inside.

'Had a good time, did you?' he asked, showing his nicotine-stained teeth as his lip curled into what he probably thought was a smile. 'Go straight through to the cloakroom and leave your boots and coats there. No dirty boots on the stairs.'

'He's worse than my mum,' said Mia to her friend Olivia.

'Shh, he'll tell you off,' replied Olivia.

'Keep moving,' called Aidan. 'That is, if you want biscuits!' Moving faster now, the group soon sorted out their outdoor clothes before going into the dining room. The urns stood ready, and the hatch door was open.

'I'll try some Welsh,' said Gavin. 'See what we get.'

'*Helo, sut wyt ti,*' he called through the hatch. A startled face looked at him.

'Please?' It was the same girl, looking more worried than yesterday.

'Ah, sorry, thought you were Welsh. Do you speak English?' Gavin asked.

'No,' she replied, looking down at her hands.

'That's OK,' said Gavin. 'Can we have some biscuits?' and he mimed eating.

'Ah, yes,' and once again she pulled some packets out of a cupboard and gave them to him.

'Thanks. What's your name?'

'Name?' she repeated.

'Gavin,' said Gavin, pointing to himself. 'You?' he asked, pointing to her.

'No,' she said, shaking her head and closing the door to the hatch.

'Well,' said Gavin, sitting with his colleagues at one of the long tables. 'Success with the biscuits, but no luck with Welsh. I don't know what nationality she is. She claims not to speak any English, and she's either putting up a good pretence or she really doesn't know any.'

'How strange to have someone working here who doesn't speak any English or Welsh,' said Freya.

'Maybe she's a refugee?' suggested Nadia. 'We'll have to ask Morgan.'

'Hmm, we'll probably find talking to kitchen staff is out of bounds too,' said Aidan. Uneasily, the others laughed their agreement.

'How did your group get on? Did everyone walk behind the waterfall?' asked Gavin.

'They did. The path was a bit slippery, but it was amazing to stand behind the water. I think they were all impressed,' said Nadia.

'It was flowing well. There must have been a lot of rain here recently. Nadia nearly got stuck in the mud. The kids thought it was hilarious,' said Aidan.

'It wasn't that funny,' said Nadia. 'My boots are caked with it. It smells, too.'

'You're going to have to risk getting your nails dirty if you want clean boots,' said Freya.

Nadia scowled. 'I know,' she said.

'It's all right, Nadia. I've got to do mine, so I may as well do yours. That last jammie dodger is mine though,' said Aidan.

'Deal,' said Nadia. 'I really don't know why you like those disgusting biscuits so much.'

It was no good. The narrow bed was lumpy, and dipped in the middle. It wasn't only the bed that made it impossible for Aidan to sleep. The place unsettled him, and the girl in the kitchen worried him. Was she as scared as she looked? Or was she just worried about her lack of English? He turned over, pulling the pillow under his head and shoulder, before turning over the other way. *I'm not going to sleep like this,* he thought. He looked at his phone. Nearly 2 am. He'd be up in just over four hours. He got up to turn on the light which flickered briefly before it went off. Aidan cursed quietly, and as though it had heard him, the light flickered back on. He found his book, and got back into bed to read.

It was windy outside, and the windows rattled with the stronger gusts. The wooden staircases and floors creaked as they eased their joints. Aidan read on, and then looked up. A different creak. A creak from a footstep. Someone was walking on the floor above him. The floor that appeared to be empty, with blacked-out windows. His senses sharpened, his book abandoned. There was a muffled yelp, and the sound of someone tripping over something, followed by silence. A long silence.

Aidan decided he must have imagined it. His book slipped from his hand, and his last thought as he drifted off to sleep was that it might have been rats. Yelping rats? It was all too confusing. Sleep drew him in, and he dreamt of rats with worried frowns that looked at him as he scrubbed a never-dwindling heap of muddy boots.

The buzzing went on, relentlessly dragging Aidan from his sleep. His swept his arm across the covers, knocking his phone to the floor. With a loud groan, he reached out to turn off the alarm, resisting the temptation to retreat deeper into the sleeping bag. He could hear the muffled voices of some of the boys, and a few shushes when the laughter threatened to get too loud. It was no good: he had to get moving.

The smell of bacon, eggs, and toast greeted Aidan when he eventually reached the dining room. Framed by the hatch window frame, Aidan noticed a new face: a red-faced woman, who was looking anxiously in his direction.

'Morning!' Aidan called cheerfully. 'Something smells good!'

The woman gave him a small smile. 'Are the kids coming down?'

Aha, she speaks English! thought Aidan. 'Yes, they'll be in any minute now,' he replied. 'I bet they'll all be starving.'

'Well, me and the girls have been cooking for a small army,' said the woman in her lilting, Welsh voice.

'I'm Aidan, by the way.'

'Carys. Carys Morgan,' said the woman.

'I tried talking to the young woman who was in the kitchen the other day, but she didn't seem to speak English.'

'That would be one of my helpers. They're just visiting,' said Carys.

'I've only met one. Where are they from?'

'There's two of them—sisters they are, from eastern Europe. Don't ask me where exactly. I just keep them busy. Now, if you'll excuse me, I'd better get on. There's only me on duty now—the girls are doing other chores for Morgan.'

'Let me know if we can do anything to help,' said Aidan.

'If you would just remind the children to stack up their dirty plates, and put the cutlery in the basket, that'll be great,' she said, closing the hatch door and ending the conversation.

The door to the dining room burst open as the first group of children rushed in to claim their breakfast.

'I'm starving!' said Noah.

'Me too,' said Olivia.

'OK kids, start helping yourselves to cereal and drinks. There's only one person working in the kitchen now so just be patient.'

More children arrived, and the initial noise settled to a low hubbub of chatter, accompanied by the scraping of spoons. The hatch window opened, and plates of bacon and eggs appeared.

Gavin, Freya, and Aidan tucked into platefuls of cooked breakfast, while Nadia pushed her spoon around a bowl of soggy-looking cereal.

'Come on, Nadia, you'll need more than that if you're going to survive the abseiling today,' said Gavin.

'Yes, mum,' said Nadia. 'If you must know, I'm worried I'm going to be ill.'

'What, do you feel ill?' asked Freya.

'Not yet. But swinging on the end of a rope might change that,' said Nadia.

'Don't worry about it. If you stay at the bottom, you won't have to abseil. I can be at the top, and get down if a child needs help,' said Aidan.

Nadia smiled at him gratefully. 'I think I can cope with that,' she said.

'Good. Best we get a move on—the mini buses will be here in

about 30 minutes.' Aidan clapped his hands to get the children's attention, before reminding them to make sure they had the right shoes and clothing with them.

'That was a laugh,' said Todd, throwing himself onto his bed. 'Does anyone else ache?'

'Yep,' said Mikey. 'We've had a good workout! Thought abseiling would be just sliding down a rope.'

'It was, but it wasn't exactly like a slide at the park, was it,' said Noah.

'Hope there's something good for supper,' said Freddie.

'All you think about is food,' said Todd. 'What do you make of this place?'

'Bit spooky,' said Noah.

'How about exploring a bit—after dark, when the teachers have gone to bed?' asked Todd.

'You'll be in trouble if you're caught,' said Freddie.

'So we won't get caught,' said Todd. 'Who's in? Mikey, Noah, Charlie … Freddie?'

'I'll be on guard,' said Freddie.

'OK,' said Todd. 'What about the rest of you?' The boys nodded cautiously.

'Right, let's get down for supper. We'll say we're tired and we'll go to bed early. Hopefully the teachers are knackered too, and they won't stay up talking for hours,' said Todd.

A flick of the switch, and the room flooded with light. A quick glance at the windows reassured him that no chink of light would be visible outside. He unzipped his fleece, sweating in the moist, warm atmosphere. Walking between the rows he noticed nothing that concerned him. All was at it should be. At the doorway, he turned out the light and stepped into the passageway, ears attuned to any unexpected sound. Silence. Good. Now all he needed to do was to keep the women quiet. He didn't want anything to upset the routine. Everything was going too well for there to be any upsets now.

'I think we wore the kids out today. They're all in bed, and some are already asleep!' said Aidan. 'Anyone else for a glass of wine?' he asked, looking around at Gavin, Nadia, and Freya. 'Anyone up for the nightclub?'

There was a groan from the other three. 'I hope that's one of your jokes, Aidan,' said Nadia. 'I'm not sure I'm capable of getting upstairs to bed, let alone dancing the night away.'

'Just as well we're in the middle of nowhere, in that case,' said Aidan.

'What's happening tomorrow? Are we all going kayaking?' asked Freya.

'Yes. We're booked in with a centre that can take all the kids. They've got enough instructors to cope, apparently,' said Aidan.

'Just as well,' said Gavin. 'I haven't seen much in the way of equipment here.'

Nadia put her emptied glass down on the table. 'Well, I'm off to get some beauty sleep. See you all at breakfast.'

'I'm just going to make sure the boys really are asleep, after that little prank with Charlie this morning,' said Aidan.

'Top up, Freya?' asked Gavin. Freya accepted, and the two sat in companionable silence, sipping wine, and yawning from time to time.

'Think I'm going to have to give in and get some sleep,' said Freya, just as the door burst open and Aidan came in.

'They're not in their beds!' said Aidan, looking worried. 'Where the hell have they got to this time?'

'Who's missing?' asked Gavin.

'Charlie, Freddie, Noah, Todd, and Mikey,' said Aidan. 'They've rolled up their clothes to make it look as though they were in bed but it was obvious what they'd done.'

'OK,' said Gavin. 'How about Freya checks on the girls' rooms to make sure they're all there, and I'll check the rest of the house. Do you want to check outdoors, Aidan? My bet is that they're trying to get into the tower.'

'Sounds a plan. Let's meet back here in fifteen minutes. Got your phones? They might be useful as torches, even if we haven't got a signal to call each other.'

'Actually, the signal seems pretty good on my phone. Might not be reliable though. See you in fifteen. Gavin, if you start on this floor, I'll come down after I've checked the girls to help you with the rest of the house.'

Aidan grabbed his coat from the storeroom and unlocked the front door, leaving it on the catch. As his eyes adjusted to the darkness, he noticed how few lights were on in the hostel, and how brightly the moon shone in the cloudless sky. He shivered, pulling up his collar. Shrubs and trees loomed up at him in the still darkness. No wind. No car noise. No animals. Time to move.

He turned left out of the front door, using the pathway to pass by the windows of the front rooms. He looked up at the dark windows of the tower, and back down to ground level. Nothing. Not a movement, not a sound. Where were they?

Carrying on to the back of the house, he discovered the path gave way to grass. Suddenly a light shone out from the top floor and Aidan instinctively stepped back to stand against the wall, in the shadow of the house. After a few minutes the light went off, and Aidan continued his circumnavigation. The ground was softer now, slightly giving way under Aidan's feet. He was just fumbling for his phone to put on the torch when he heard a stifled giggle.

'Charlie, Freddie, is that you?' hissed Aidan, trying not to make too much noise. There was silence, then an abrupt yelp and some squelching sounds. Torch now on, he tried to see where the boys were but couldn't see anything. Aidan picked his way carefully over the muddy ground, hoping to find them.

'Noah? Noah?' heard Aidan, followed by some muffled screams that sounded genuinely frightened.

'Noah, stop messing around and get back here.' That was Freddie's voice.

'Noah? Noah? You OK?' A worried voice, probably Mikey's.

'What the hell do you think you're doing?' asked Aidan as he finally reached the boys. A dip in the ground and the lack of light had been enough to hide them from his view.

'Mr Wilcox!' exclaimed Charlie. 'We can't find Noah! I think he's fallen down somewhere.'

'Is everyone else here? Mikey, Todd, Charlie, Freddie? Just Noah then,' said Aidan. 'We'll have to call him—Noah! Noah! Keep quiet, boys, so we can hear if he answers.'

There was a muffled answer, and Aidan swung his torch in the direction it came from.

'Good … grief,' said Aidan, managing to keep a check on his choice of expletive. 'You're covered in mud!'

'Get me out of here!' whimpered Noah. 'I can't do it on my own.' Noah wrapped his arms around his body, shivering, as he stood thigh-deep in mud. Brown streaks covered his coat, and his front and face bore witness to having fallen in, face first.

'I'm not surprised,' said Aidan, looking more closely at the expanse of mud. It looked like an old pond where the earth had built up over time, with the winter rains turning the soil to thick mud. He looked around for something to stand on so he could get closer to the edge to help Noah out. Stacked against an outbuilding were some old planks. 'OK, Noah, we'll get you out, but I don't want anyone else to fall in so we're going to have to be careful how we rescue you. Understand?'

'Yes, Mr Wilcox,' said Noah, sounding relieved now that rescue seemed possible.

'Right, Charlie, give me a hand with one of these planks. Mikey, Todd, and Freddie, I want you right out of the way.'

'Come away from the window,' hissed Cristina. 'Someone will see you.' There was just enough moonlight to see the interior of the room: the curtains, with their faded pattern, and the dark carpet that felt slightly sticky to the touch. There was not much space for both of them. If one of them sat on the bed, the other had to sit on the floor. But Elena persisted in standing close to the window.

'Good. I'm bored with hiding away. That man today was friendly, but I had to be rude. I hate it,' said Elena.

'It won't be for much longer.'

'How do you know?' There was no reply. 'Should we try to escape?'

'How can we?' replied Cristina with her back against the iron frame of the bed. 'We don't exist. We've no papers, no passports. Where would we go?'

'So we just do nothing? We can't even go home!' wailed Elena. 'Wait, there's that nice teacher.'

'Don't wave to him, you little fool!' Cristina's voice was sharp, even at a whisper.

'I wasn't going to. I'm not stupid.'

Cristina raised her eyebrows. 'Come, eat the biscuits Carys made,' she said, patting a space on the bed. 'There is just room on the bed for you if you don't fidget too much.'

Elena moved to sit on the bed. 'What are these things with raisins in that Carys is always making? They're not cake, and they're too soft for biscuits. This is such a weird country.'

'Best try to get used to it. It's our home for now. At least we're still together,' said Cristina.

'I can't believe Uncle Marius told us we'd have a wonderful life here,' said Elena.

Aidan, with Charlie's help, manoeuvred one plank into place, then another, wondering if these would be enough for Noah to get himself out. Aidan gingerly walked out onto a plank, which dipped with his weight. *I'll have to lie down,* he thought. He eased himself onto his front, and wriggled his way towards Noah.

'Noah, are your feet on the bottom of the mud? Can you move yourself forward, towards me?'

Noah pushed forward, the mud clinging greedily to his legs. Slowly, he inched closer towards the edge of the pond.

'Is it any firmer now?' asked Aidan.

'Noooo …. Oh, there's something here. I think there's a ledge. I'll try …. I'll try to get on to it.' Noah squelched his way slowly forwards, the mud sucking at his thighs. Eventually Noah dragged himself up onto the ledge that was hidden in the mud.

'Put your arms out, towards me. I'll hold onto your forearms. See if you can move yourself more onto the ledge. That's it,' said Aidan, as Noah moved another inch forward. 'Can you move a bit more?'

With an expression of concentration rarely seen in the classroom, Noah moved slowly onto the ledge. Aidan wriggled back on the plank. 'Now,' said Aidan, 'can you lean onto the plank, and haul yourself out? I'll try to keep hold of you so you won't slide back in again.'

Grunting and groaning, Noah pushed himself onto the plank while Aidan hauled on Noah's shoulders. With his hands now covered in slimy, smelly mud, Aidan's grip on Noah loosened, and he feared Noah would slip back into the pond. With a huge effort, Aidan clung on to Noah's coat.

'Right, put everything you've got into it. You're nearly there,' said Aidan, trying to ignore the stench of the mud. Another groan, and the stinking mud reluctantly gave Noah up. He was on the plank, tears washing channels down his muddied cheeks.

'Thanks, Mr Wilcox. You saved my life.'

His friends gave a ragged cheer, and Aidan quickly shushed them. 'I might have saved your life, but it won't be worth living if we can't get back inside without being seen. Noah, you'll walk with me. Todd, take my phone and use the torch so we can see where we're going. Keep the beam pointing down, and let's hope we can get back in without anyone seeing us.'

'Yuk, you smell, Noah. Mr Wilcox, does he have to share our room?'

'Shhh. He'll be all right once he's had a shower. I'll have to work out what to do with his clothes.'

'You're useless, Freddie. You were supposed to be on lookout,' said Todd.

'If you were left by that spooky house on your own, you'd do a runner too,' said Freddie.

'Would not,' said Todd.

'Shhh – we need to be absolutely silent,' said Aidan.

'How much longer are those girls with us?'

'No idea. Until Marius says they can go home, I suppose.'

'It's been nearly a year! Surely you've done enough for that man.'

'Stop your whinging, woman. He is paying us.'

'Not a lot though. It barely covers their keep. And the longer they're here, the more of a risk it is. People expect us to be friendly, and it looks weird when the girls can't say anything.'

'You'll have to think of something then, won't you?' said Morgan, rolling a cigarette.

'It's been long enough. And the girls are restless. They don't want to be here either.'

'Stop nagging me, won't you. There's nothing I can do about it.' Morgan got up, and banged out of the back door.

When would life ever return to the way it was—before Morgan went on the skiing holiday? thought Carys.

It was a quiet group that walked slowly back to Alwyn Hall after the mud rescue. A light shone out from the hallway, but otherwise the place was in darkness.

'Mikey, try to open the front door quietly. You might find Mr Davies in the hall.'

Mikey pushed open the door, jumping when Gavin said 'Thank God, we were wondering what could have happened.'

'Thought you were Morgan,' said Mikey, looking scared.

The boys followed Mikey inside, with Aidan and Noah last.

'Where have you been? What's that stink? You're covered in mud!' exclaimed Gavin.

'It's a long story,' said Aidan. 'I'll join you when I've got Noah and me cleaned up, and the boys really are in bed this time.'

'I made tea—is that OK?' asked Gavin. 'You'd probably prefer a double brandy but we forgot to bring any. Well, I forgot.'

'Tea's great, thanks, and no, I didn't bring any brandy either,' said Aidan, easing himself into a chair. 'What a night! I can't believe we escaped the wrath of Morgan.'

'What did they think they were doing?' asked Gavin.

'It was just a prank—you know how it goes: there's a rule about not wandering around outside which immediately makes them want to do exactly that, especially when there's a tower to investigate. Apparently they found the tower was locked, so they looked around the back of the house, veered off a bit to the right, and then Noah ended up in an old pond that was full of really smelly mud. I don't think any of them will be venturing out again.'

'Good thing you went to check on them,' said Gavin. 'It's a strange old place. We had a good look round it but you can't get onto the top floor—the door to the top corridor is locked. I could have sworn someone was up there though. I thought I heard footsteps, and a light switch click. Maybe that's where Morgan sleeps when he's on duty.'

'The whole place feels a bit weird. I thought I heard someone up on the top floor last night so you might be right about Morgan. Do you know what I'm thinking?'

'What?' asked Gavin. 'More tea?'

'No. That all this would make a good setting for a story. Something a bit spooky, or a fantasy.'

'You sure you didn't sneak a slug of brandy into that tea?' asked Gavin.

Aidan laughed. 'Wish I could have done! Well, I think I'll turn in now and get some sleep—what's left of the night! Apart from the locked upper floor, did you find anything else when you looked around the house?'

'Only the washing machines, which you're using. We didn't go into the rooms marked private, just in case we found Morgan in his pjs.'

'On that note,' said Aidan with a grimace, 'I'm off. See you later.'

'They've left,' said Cristina as she came into her sister's bedroom. Cristina slept in an even smaller room, next door.

'Who? Not Morgan?' asked Elena. 'He can't leave.'

'No, the nice guy with the school kids. We're stuck with just Morgan and Carys again, until another school group arrives. Or we have to make another delivery.'

'When will that be? It's not exactly busy, is it?' asked Elena. 'Not for school trips or for deliveries.'

'No idea. We'll have to wait and see. Shhh, I can hear footsteps,' said Cristina.

The girls fell silent and listened as the footsteps got closer, stopping outside their door.

Cristina opened the door and looked along the passageway. Morgan was unlocking the door at the end.

'How is everything? You are keeping them warm?' she asked him.

'Everything's good. Growing well. As it should do with all this heat. Have you heard from your uncle?'

'No. I will tell you when he gives us our next job.'

February 2023

Aidan sat on the stool in his kitchen and jotted down a few notes for what he hoped would be the starting point for a story. Why did Alwyn Hall have such an unfriendly atmosphere? Why were there so many locked doors? And what was Morgan worried about? Apart from the boggy mud, surely there couldn't be any other dangers that made it necessary to ban exploring the grounds? He might never find the answers, but he could use the sense of foreboding for a new story.

The last few days at Alwyn Hall had gone quickly and without mishap, and the teachers had handed back thirty tired but happy children to their respective parents with a sense of relief.

The characters and the plot for a story slowly started to take shape in Aidan's mind. By the end of the summer term, he had written a first draft.

July, 2023

Aidan walked into the staffroom of the primary school where he worked as a teacher, and greeted his visitors. He'd booked an author and illustrator to talk to the children about story writing, hoping it would be a fun activity for the end of term.

'Hi, I'm Aidan, and you must be Becca and Jen. It's great to meet you both!' said Aidan. 'The children are in the hall, so if you've finished your coffee I'll take you through and introduce you.'

'Thanks, Aidan, yes, we're all set,' said Jen, picking up her flipchart and adjusting the straps of her colourful dungarees. 'Did you manage to get a stand for this to go on?'

'Yes, it's set up for you. I assume you've got pens, or whatever you need?' said Aidan. Jen nodded.

'Becca, how about you?' asked Aidan.

'All I need are these copies of my books to show to the children. I'll be talking to the kids and encouraging them to come up with ideas to make a story, and Jen will do the drawing to go with it,' replied Becca.

'Sounds fun. The children are really excited to meet you,' said Aidan, opening the door to the hall. There was a faint smell of school lunches, and a buzz of expectant voices which quietened a little as Aidan led his guests in.

'OK, everyone, I'd like you to welcome our visitors …'.

The children applauded enthusiastically. Working with Becca and Jen, they had created a funny story, brought to life with Jen's drawings. As the children returned to their classrooms, Jen and Becca headed back to the staffroom for a cup of tea, and to talk with Aidan.

'That was great,' said Aidan. 'They really got stuck in—and it worked well creating the story through both words and pictures.'

'Thanks—we enjoyed it,' said Jen. 'Working with children like this means a lot to us, because when we start planning a new story we've got a good idea of what kids like, or don't like!'

'Yes, I can see that. Story writing isn't as easy as people might think.'

'Do you write, Aidan?' asked Becca.

'Well, just for fun. I've never tried to get anything published,' said Aidan.

'What sort of things do you write?' asked Jen.

'Oh, children's stories mostly. I got the idea for the last one from a residential trip I went on with Year 6—the ten- and eleven-year-olds.'

'What's it about?' asked Becca.

'Well, in the story, the kids get sucked into a superswamp, a fantasy world where they face lots of challenges. The reader has to choose what the kids in story will do next. I've given them some options to choose from. Some options prove to be good choices, others make things even trickier. It's a bit complicated, but I think I've got a reasonable first draft now,' explained Aidan.

'I love that idea,' said Jen. 'It would make a really good graphic novel. When you've finished it, why don't you send it to Phoenix Publishing? I know they're looking for new authors, and you don't have to go through an agent.'

‘Gosh, OK, I’ll think about it. I’ll have to give it a bit of a polish first though!’ laughed Aidan. ‘It’s a good thing the summer holidays are coming up!’

August 2023

He read it. He re-wrote parts, and wrote them yet again. He nearly despaired. But finally, just before the start of the new school year, Aidan felt he was as ready as he could be to show *Superswamp—get us out!* to Phoenix Publishing.

Weeks later, pushing the trolley around his local supermarket, Aidan's phone buzzed. Juggling the packet of mushrooms he'd just picked up he took the call, answering 'Hello? Oh yes, hello.' There was a pause, followed by a whoop of excitement from Aidan.

'Really, dear, I know they've got a yellow sticker but is it necessary to make all that noise?' asked a startled, elderly shopper.

'Sorry, yes, no, oh it's not the sticker, it's ….' Aidan gave up trying to explain. 'Sorry,' he said to the caller, 'I'm in the supermarket. Look, I'm really pleased you want to make me an offer but can I call you back?'

Checking his emails the following morning, his eyes went straight to one from Amy Chang, Phoenix Publishing. His finger hovered over it. Had he dreamed it? Did Phoenix really want his book? He tapped, and the email opened, confirming yesterday's call with Amy, and the details of the offer for his first book.

Don't think I'll give up the day job just yet, he thought, looking at the financial part of the offer. *But it's not about the money. I'm going to be published!*

Reading on, the next step meant setting up a call with Amy to talk about the book, and the illustrations. *Wouldn't it be great if Jen could do the drawings!* thought Aidan.

Talking to Amy later in the week, Aidan asked about potential illustrators.

'We thought Jen Somerville would be a good choice, if she's got time,' said Amy.

'Perfect! I saw her drawings when she came to give a talk at school, and I think her style would work really well for *Superswamp*. And I think we'd work well together, too,' said Aidan.

By the October half-term holiday, Jen was ready to start working with Aidan and Amy on the book.

'How did you get the idea for *Superswamp*?' Jen asked. 'Didn't you say it was a school trip?'

'It was,' said Aidan.

'Hope it wasn't like the one in your story!' commented Amy.

'No, but there was something odd about the place—and one of the boys did end up stuck in some mud one night. He went exploring after dark with some of his friends which was strictly forbidden.'

'Forbidden? That sounds a bit harsh! I thought these places were all about getting the kids out of their comfort zones and doing outdoor stuff,' said Jen.

'I know, that's what I was expecting. Apparently there was a lot of maintenance going on—not that we saw any. More like putting out the cones on a motorway and leaving them for months!'

'Was it a good time for the kids, and the staff?' asked Jen.

'I think everyone felt uneasy there. We were all a bit nervous of the place, and I suddenly thought it would make a good setting for a story—and *Superswamp* came from that.'

'Hey, would it be possible to book in for a night? Or is it school groups only?' asked Jen. 'It would be great to go there and pick up on the vibes.'

'Good idea. I'll find out and let you know,' said Aidan.

March 2024

Aidan's phone pinged. It was a message that could wait until later. He'd spent longer than he'd realised, reliving his time at Alwyn Hall. Fortunately, it was a Saturday or he would have been late for school. *To hell with them, whoever they are* thought Aidan. *This book is going to be published*. Feeling more purposeful now the letter was in the bin and he'd finished his coffee, Aidan cleared a space on the rickety table that served as his desk. It was a dumping ground for books he was reading, schoolbooks that needed marking, and any other paperwork he intended to read when he had time. *Time—that would be a treat*, he thought. His days were busy with teaching at his local primary school, his evenings comprised of marking and preparing for the next day, and any spare time was spent writing—or thinking about writing.

He opened his laptop. He'd already downloaded the document that would become his first book. His first published book! If it hadn't involved so much work it might feel like a dream. He looked through each page carefully, checking that the illustrations and text worked together. Each chapter ended with two or three options for the reader to choose the next stage of the story, and these also needed checking to make sure they all worked. He'd gone through this countless times already, with Amy and with Jen, but this was his very last chance to spot any problems before the book appeared in print, or on a screen as an e-book.

His stomach rumbled. Aidan realised he hadn't eaten since the morning, and it was now dark outside. He wrote a quick email to Amy and Jen, telling them about the few details that he'd picked up on, and confirming he understood these were final changes before publishing. There was a new email from Amy, which he opened. Phoenix Publishing was offering him a contract for a series of books. Shocked, he sat back in his chair as conflicting thoughts tumbled through his mind. *Wow! Amazing! Can I write more? What if I get writer's block? What about that letter?*

He quickly sent a reply to Amy saying how excited he was at the offer. He needed a beer, and someone to talk it all through with before accepting. Instinctively, he found himself texting Jen.

Jen's snore woke her with a jolt. Her throat felt a bit sore, and her mouth was parched dry. She opened her eyes, and blinked at the light sneaking out around the edges of the bedroom curtains. Last night had been great, getting together with her old friend Sam Holliday, but she'd lost count of the number of times they'd topped up their wine glasses. *Oh well, best get it over and done with*, she thought, as she swung her legs carefully over the side of the bed before making the short walk to the bathroom.

Checking her phone, she picked up a text from Sam, and another from Aidan Wilcox. *Got some good news to share with you. Fancy a beer soon?* Jen wasn't sure when she'd be ready to face alcohol ever again. Not until she'd had at least three cups of coffee.

Showered, dressed, and coffee cup in hand, she arranged to meet Aidan that evening. An email popped up from Amy at Phoenix Publishing. *How are you fixed with work over the next 12-24 months? May be commissioning more books like Superswamp. Talk soon?*

Wonder if Aidan knows about that? thought Jen. *Perhaps that's Aidan's good news?* She finished her coffee, and switched on her computer to look at the final proofs of *Superswamp*.

Beers in hand, Aidan weaved his way through the crowded bar to the table where Jen waited.

'Here's to *Superswamp,'* she said, raising her glass to clink against his. 'I looked at the proofs today. It's going to be brilliant. Alwyn Hall might have been weird, but it definitely inspired a great storyline! Remember our visit there?'

'How could I forget? It was just as odd as the first time I went there with the school. And yes … yes, *Superswamp* is great. You've really brought the story to life with your drawings. You're very clever, Jen,' replied Aidan.

'I sense a but. What's up? We both know it's a great story, and Sam will do a good job with the marketing.'

'I know,' sighed Aidan, looking into his glass of beer.

'So why the long face?'

'Don't get me wrong. It's not the book. Well, not the book itself. It's …. well, I had this letter.'

'Asking you to write more?'

Aidan laughed. 'I have got the offer of a contract for more books. But that's not what I meant. I got this anonymous letter …'

'Right … that doesn't sound good,' said Jen. 'What did it say?'

'Not much. '*Kill the book or we kill you.*' That's all.'

'What?' yelped Jen, startling the people closest to the table. 'What! Say that again?'

'Kill the book or we'll kill you.'

'Jumping jellybeans! Oh sorry, it's just something we say in my family,' said Jen in response to Aidan's quizzical expression. 'And you've got no idea who this letter is from? Have you told the police?'

'Er, no.'

'What have you done with it?'

'Um, I threw it in the bin.' The expression on Jen's face told him that hadn't been the smartest of moves. 'Well, it was horrible. I felt almost—well, contaminated by it. I just wanted it out of sight. And now Phoenix are about to go to print, and they want me to write more books.'

Jen sighed. 'What a cowardly thing to do. No, not throwing it in the bin. I meant sending a letter like that. Who could have done it?'

'I've been wracking my brains about that. It's almost as though someone feels threatened by the book. But why? And who? People at school know about it, but they're all really pleased for me. Family and friends know and there's no problem with any of them. I'm just going to hope it's some kind of sick joke, and that's all there is to it.'

'I've told a few friends about it too, but no-one's going to be that paranoid about it being published. If it is a joke, it's a pretty sick one.'

Aidan sipped his beer. 'Let's talk about something else. What have you been up to?'

'Well, I met up with Sam last night.'

'Oh great. How's she doing?'

'All right. Her uncle died recently, so she's got the funeral to go to. Think it was a bit of a shock, but she's all right otherwise.'

The two sides of the curtain glided together, as though moved by an invisible hand. Juddering on the curve of the rail, the two halves finally joined. It was over. Uncertain of the etiquette, Sam looked around to follow the lead of someone who knew what to do. People in the front row rose unsteadily to their feet, reluctant to lead the way out and yet unable to resist the gentle encouragement of the celebrant to leave. No one wanted to move. No one wanted to stay. But the allocated time had elapsed, and the next funeral would soon begin.

Sam stepped into the watery sunshine, a little unsteady on unfamiliar heels, clutching her bag and blinking in surprise at its brightness. It wouldn't have surprised her if it was already twilight. Looking around, she caught the eye of one or two people she recognised, exchanging slight smiles that were held in check by the solemnity of the occasion.

'There you are, Sam,' said her mother, Elaine, looking smart in a navy-blue jacket and coordinating dress. An older woman, swamped in a black coat with an over-sized brooch was clinging to Elaine's arm. 'You remember Aunt Mildred, of course.'

The Aunt Mildred Sam remembered would have comfortably filled the coat at one time, but the brooch, and the slightly worried expression on the face above it, were very familiar. 'Of course I do,' said Sam. 'It's … well, I'm glad to see you, although it's a sad day for all of us.'

'My dear, I've got to the age where funerals outnumber the weddings. It is sad, but remember, my brother—your Uncle Harry—lived a good life, even if he did end sooner than any of us expected. He was still rattling around in that campervan of his, and he was still planning trips for this summer.'

'He loved his camper, didn't he,' Sam agreed.

'He would have liked a gypsy-style funeral. You know, where they burn the wagon with the coffin in it,' said Aunt Mildred.

'Do they really?' asked Sam. 'I thought that was only in *Peaky Blinders*.'

'Well, maybe not at a Cotswolds Crematorium,' said Aunt Mildred, looking worried at the thought.

'Come on,' said Elaine, 'let's get to the hotel and have something to eat.' She drew Aunt Mildred towards a waiting car. 'You can come with us, if you like, Sam. Your father's driving, and there's a spare seat.'

'Great, thanks, I'll do that,' said Sam, falling into step behind them. It was going to be a long afternoon, fending off the inevitable questions from older family members about her unmarried status. Just past forty, she had a good career in marketing, but some older family members would still want to see her 'settled' with the stability of a husband. Squaring her shoulders, she helped Aunt Mildred into the front seat before getting into the back with her mother.

'All set?' asked David, turning round to check on his wife and daughter before reversing out of the parking space.

The key turned easily in the lock, and Sam stepped into the peaceful silence of her sitting room. Clicking on the lamp, she let out a sigh of relief. Her own space. Her choice to play music or not. And no need to talk, at least not for now. She busied herself drawing curtains and putting away her coat before going into the kitchen to pour a glass of wine.

She selected some gentle jazz—a singer she'd discovered only recently. The house felt warm and welcoming, a haven from the sadness of the funeral and the social requirements of the wake. Glass in hand, she picked up a photo of her parents with Uncle Harry. Harry was younger than his sister, Mildred, but a good ten years older than her father. Always a free spirit, travelling across Europe and even North Africa with his campervan throughout his sixties and seventies. She remembered him from her childhood, turning up at family celebrations, always looking a bit dishevelled but always with an idea for a game, or a story to tell. *He should have had longer*, she thought. *But at least he lived life to the full—and full of the things he enjoyed most.* She raised her glass to the photo *May the wheels keep on turning, Uncle Harry, wherever you are now.*

Sam settled into the sofa, putting her feet up and getting the cushions positioned behind her back, just as she liked them. She took a sip of the crisp, dry white wine, and thought back to when she'd first moved into the house over a year ago. She struggled to remember life before she made the move, although it hadn't been easy to step away from her five-year relationship with a controlling partner. Nor had it been easy to start a new job with Little Bear, the children's book publisher. She'd been so excited that she'd be working on her favourite series, *Granny Fi*. And then came the realisation that sales had plummeted, and that there was a lot going wrong at the Little Bear company. But she'd come through it all, making new friends along the way, and even identifying who had murdered *Granny Fi's* illustrator. And now here she was, settled in her own home, with a job with Phoenix Publishing, the company that had taken over from Little Bear.

Sam looked around the meeting room table at her colleagues' familiar faces. She thought back to her first meeting at Little Bear, with Brendan McManners, the Publishing Director and also her boss; Melissa Bingley, author of the company's best-selling series *Granny Fi*; and colleagues from the design and editorial teams. A tense meeting, bordering on hostile, with everyone terrified of incurring Melissa or Brendan's wrath. Now Melissa was serving a prison sentence for murdering *Granny Fi's* illustrator, Kaye Butterworth, and Brendan had left Little Bear when his unethical approach to business was revealed.

Kaye Butterworth had founded Little Bear with her sister, Charlotte, in the 1980s. When Kaye was murdered, Charlotte decided to close the company, setting up Phoenix Publishing to replace it, with herself as Chief Executive. Charlotte's willingness to try new ideas meant the company was now firmly in the 21st century, with new authors and illustrators signed up and books available in print and as e-books.

Charlotte's brisk manner kept the agenda moving. Turning to Sam, she smiled as she said 'Sam, can you give us an update on what we've got coming out for Christmas? I know it's only March, but bookshops will be planning their stock soon, and we do want to sell print books as well as digital.'

'Sure,' said Sam. 'Aidan Wilcox's book is our lead Christmas title,' said Sam. 'I think most of you know about it, but just to remind you, it's a graphic novel aimed at the tween market—kids who are not yet teenagers, but aren't really young children either. It's set around a school residential trip, where kids stay in an away-from-it-all place. Usually, everyone has a great time. But on this trip, things start to go wrong and the kids find themselves transported into the superswamp of a fantasy world, experiencing some tricky situations. For each situation, the reader has to choose what happens next. They're given two or three options to choose from. Each option leads to a different outcome.'

'Kids will like the fantasy element, and making their own decisions,' commented Charlotte.

'Yes, I agree, I think both will have a strong appeal,' said Sam. 'As they read on, they uncover clues to help them work out *why* everything's gone wrong on this school trip, and who's behind it all. As you probably know, Jen Somerville, who used to work with me in marketing, is now a freelance illustrator. She's drawn the most amazing illustrations for the book. We should attract a new type of reader with it. I've started working on some ideas for marketing which I want to talk through with Aidan and Jen.'

Sam paused, looking through some papers. 'Here, you can get a better idea by looking at some of the page designs,' and she passed a few pages from the book around the table. 'It's going to work best as an interactive e-book, but it does also work as a print book.'

'It's brilliant,' said Charlotte, looking at the sample. 'I've got great hopes for this author. I'm hoping he's got another book in the pipeline so we've got the start of an Aidan Wilcox series. We need to build up a following of readers who want to buy every Aidan Wilcox book we can publish.'

'Do we have a contract with him for more books?' asked Jason Lee, one of the designers.

Amy Chang replied 'I emailed him the other day with the offer of a new contract for more books and I'm waiting for him to get back to me.'

'I'll leave that with you, Amy,' said Charlotte. 'Sam, update me on your marketing plans for *Superswamp* once you've met with Aidan, please. Now, what else do we have for Christmas sales?'

April 2024

Early Spring suited Lower Rushford. The daffodils were nodding in a light breeze, brightening the banks of the river Rush that flowed below the stone bridge. Splashes of colour from crocuses and narcissi brightened front gardens, and a magnolia tree presented its luscious blooms for everyone to admire. But Sam's mind was on getting home, and calling her parents.

The welcoming smell of supper greeted her as she opened the door. She'd put the slow cooker her parents had given her last Christmas to good use, leaving it to gently cook delicious suppers while she was at work. Now she took off the lid, savouring the spiciness of the sauce, and checking everything was cooked. It was ready, but she would call her parents first.

The phone rang a few times before her mother answered. 'We're fine,' Elaine said in answer to Sam's enquiry. 'A bit tired after the meeting with the solicitor. It's not the easiest drive to his office.'

'How's Dad?' asked Sam.

'Have a word with him—he's right here. You know Uncle Harry made him the executor of his will?' said Elaine.

'No, I don't think I knew that. Will there be much to do?' asked Sam.

'Hold on, here's your father. Speak to you again in a minute,' said Elaine.

'Hi Dad,' said Sam. 'OK? Mum says you're Uncle Harry's executor. What's that going to mean?'

'I'm all right, love,' said her father. 'Oh, probably working through a load of paperwork. I can't imagine Harry left things neat and tidy, but I might be proved wrong. At least he left a will, which I have a copy of. There's a surprise in it for you.'

'A nice surprise?' asked Sam.

'I think you'll be pleased. He's left you his campervan.'

'Oh my!' said Sam. 'I hadn't thought about what would happen to that. Gosh, he knew I always envied him his trips away.'

'Thought you'd like that,' said David. 'It'll be handy for going to visit your friend Nate in Cumbria, and when you go off to visit authors. Maybe even for a holiday.'

'It will be amazing. I wish Uncle Harry was still around to use it, but I'll definitely enjoy having it. Didn't he have a name for it? Hettie? Hattie?'

'It's Hattie. We could go over and have a look at her when you're free. I think Harry will have left her in good order, even if his paperwork's likely to be in a muddle!'

'I'd like that. Maybe we could go sometime over Easter? I'll have a long weekend. Perhaps we could drive over together?' suggested Sam.

'Sounds a plan,' said her father. 'Right, here's your mother again.'

Her supper eaten, Sam couldn't wait to message Nate. She'd met Nate last year while walking in the Lake District. Coming down a footpath, she'd sprained her ankle and was struggling to walk. By chance, Nate was on the same path. He'd lent her his walking poles and accompanied her back to the pub where she was staying. Sam offered to buy him a pint later that evening, and found she enjoyed his company. A former police officer, he couldn't be more different from her former partner who still worked in the police force. Nate now made a living as an author, writing about his native Cumbria. It was Nate who had found Kaye Butterworth's body, and who gave a home to Kaye's beloved dog, Gustav.

Nate's reply was almost immediate. *Exciting! Where's your first trip going to be?* he asked.

Getting it home's going to be the first thing! I've got to get used to driving it. And reversing it!!! Sam replied.

You'll be fine. How about meeting up over Easter? Nate asked.

Dad and I are going to Uncle Harry's to look at the van. Want to join us?

Sure! We can take it out to give you some practice.

Cheers! Sam signed off and smiled to herself. *Driving lessons in a campervan. Now that'll put our relationship to the test,* she thought.

Sam checked her calendar for the week. *Great,* she thought. *Meeting up with Jen again on Friday. That'll be fun.*

Amy waved the jar of coffee at Sam, who smiled and nodded as she walked into the kitchen area used by Phoenix's staff.

'I've been trying to get in touch with Aidan Wilcox, but no luck so far. Have you had any contact with him, Sam?'

'No, he's gone a bit quiet. I wanted to talk to him about *Super-swamp*. It's not urgent, but I'd like to get a plan in place soon.'

'Let me know if you hear from him. I'm hoping he's going to sign the contract to write more books with us.'

'Perhaps he's got pre-publication nerves?' asked Sam.

'Hmm, maybe. He'll have to get over them if he wants to make it as an author!'

Sam walked briskly through Lower Rushford, anticipating a quiet evening in her own company. Her phone pinged with a message from Jen. *Funny,* thought Sam. *We only met up a couple of nights ago. Maybe she needs to cancel meeting on Friday.*

At home, and with a mug of tea by her side, Sam settled on the sofa and read Jen's message. *Aidan is in a spot of bother. We need to talk. Might be easier face-to-face. See you in the pub at 8?*

Sam sighed. Fond as she was of Jen, the thought of turning out again didn't appeal, not even for a glass of wine. Even the word 'wine' made her feel slightly queasy, thinking back to her last evening with Jen. But Jen wouldn't ask to meet her without good reason. She sent a quick reply to confirm, and then set about warming some soup and changing into more casual clothes. At least the wood-burning stove would be going at the pub: the evenings still had a chill to them in early Spring.

'Hi, Jen,' said Sam, spotting her friend already seated at a table. 'How's things?' she asked, giving Jen a quick hug.

'All right, but I'm worried about Aidan. I've got lots to tell you, but let's get something to drink. My round,' said Jen.

'Thanks. I'll have a glass of sauvignon blanc, please. Better make it a small one.'

Sitting comfortably in low-backed armchairs, the two women took their first sips of wine and relaxed, enjoying the glowing warmth of the woodburning stove.

'So, what's all this stuff you've got to tell me? Let me guess: you've met someone? You've got a new project? You've won the lottery?'

'No, no, and no,' said Jen, smiling. 'It's, well, it's all about Aidan.'

'Aha,' said Sam. 'Don't tell me: you're finally an item?'

'What? No, don't be daft. We work together, and I count him as a friend. And now he's a friend in a spot of bother.'

'How do you mean?' asked Sam.

'He received a letter, an anonymous one, with a really horrible message.'

'What, Aidan? I can't imagine anyone wanting to be horrible to him. Unless it's a disgruntled parent?'

'No, I don't think so. It's from someone who doesn't want the book published. *Kill the book or we kill you*, the message said.'

'That's … well, that's just sick,' said Sam, frowning. 'Why would anyone want to do that?'

'That's the million-dollar question. If we knew the answer to that, we'd know who'd written it.'

'Has he gone to the police?'

'No, he just binned it, but it's clearly got to him. That's why he hasn't accepted Phoenix's contract for more books.'

There was a pause while Sam tried to absorb what Jen had just told her. A few sips of wine later Sam asked 'Do you think he'd talk to me about it?'

'He might do. I could ask him. He'll be breaking up for the Easter holidays soon, so he might have a bit more time.'

'Yes. I assume he hasn't told anyone at Phoenix?'

'No. I think he only told me because he's worried, and doesn't know what to do about the new contract.'

'You don't think he'll pull out of publishing *Superswamp*, do you?'

Jen looked at Sam, and noted her frown. 'No, he wants to go ahead. He's put too much work into it to be fobbed off by an anonymous letter. But it is a bit unnerving. Don't mention it to anyone at work, will you?'

'No, I'll speak to Aidan first. I can either get in touch to talk about the marketing of his book and hope he tells me about the letter, or you could ask him if he'd talk to me about it. What do you think?'

'Hmm,' Jen sipped her wine. 'I think—I think I'll ask him if he'll talk to you. Maybe the three of us can come up with something between us. No idea what though.'

'OK. Message me and let me know what he says. Oh, that reminds me. I've got some news too. Quite exciting news,' said Sam, smiling.

'You've got a new job? Nate's proposed?' asked Jen, looking much brighter.

'Nothing like that. No, Uncle Harry's left me his campervan in his will, and I'm going to have a look at it over Easter with Nate and my dad.'

'What fun! A campervan—wow! I can just see you cavorting

around the countryside, interviewing authors and having a great time. Do you think Nate will go with you?'

'He sounded keen, so let's hope Gustav will approve.' Gustav was Kaye Butterworth's dog. Nate had taken care of him after Kaye's death, and he'd stayed with Nate ever since.

'He'll love it. He'll have you two wrapped around his great big paws. Bet you he claims most of the bed space!'

'You could be right there! Now, another glass? My round,' said Sam.

The two sisters sat in silence. Elena sat on the floor with her back to the bed, picking at fluff on the carpet. Her fingers moved constantly, and she sniffed as she picked at the carpet. Cristina lay on the bed, her eyes closed.

'Stop it, Elena, you're driving me mad!' cried Cristina.

'I just want to go home,' said Elena, thumping the carpet to accentuate each word.

'So do I,' replied Cristina. 'But there's another delivery to do tomorrow, and then it's back to the kitchen again.'

'I'm not doing it,' said Elena. 'I won't. You can't make me.'

Cristina sat up. 'No, I can't, but think about what that will mean if we don't. We know too much. We've got no papers, no passports. We're prisoners.'

Elena sighed. 'I know. But we can't spend the rest of our lives here! We're too young. I want to go home.'

'Home to Uncle Marius? I'd rather die here,' said Cristina. 'Even if we get home we'd still have to work for him, or for our father. Don't forget Marius has kept our passports. Remember, he said we had to work for him here until he says we've paid off the cost of getting us to the UK. Then we can find our 'dream jobs,' whatever that might mean.'

'We may as well be prisoners. We've no freedom whether we're here or home in Romania,' said Elena. 'We need a plan. We have to get out of this place, and away from Uncle Marius.'

'We can't leave here without our passports,' insisted Cristina. 'We'd end up in a detention centre.'

'We came into the UK legally though. Honestly, you're such a pessimist, Cristina,' said Elena. 'There must be something we can do.'

'I'm a realist,' Cristina replied. 'And we need to think very carefully before we do anything.'

Sam woke with a start. She was about to throw herself on top of a pile of books to prevent them being run over by a large SUV. The alarm that she usually thought of as calm and tuneful jangled annoyingly in her ears. Well, at least she hadn't been run over. And the books were safe. It was just a dream—an anxiety dream, and no prizes for guessing what had triggered it. *Who would want to kill Aidan's book, or Aidan?* Sam wondered for the umpteenth time.

The day passed quickly enough, with plenty of work. It felt easier to stay at her desk and keep busy, and reduce the chance of bumping in to Amy with questions about Aidan.

Checking her phone again, she was relieved to see a message from Aidan. *Jen got in touch. Yes, fine to call me. We can talk about the letter if you want.*

I'll call you later, from home, Sam replied.

Closing the front door behind her, Sam turned on a lamp and waited for the feeling of peace that she usually felt on arriving home. But this evening it wasn't there. If anything, the furnishings almost felt accusing. *Oh for heavens sake,* thought Sam. *Yes, I'm going to make the call. Then perhaps I can settle down to a quiet evening.*

Tea made, Sam made herself comfortable on the sofa with phone, notebook, and pen at the ready. She found Aidan in her contacts. *Video call? No, maybe a bit intrusive,* she thought. The ring tone sounded twice, and Aidan answered with a quiet 'Hi, Sam.'

'Aidan, how are you? I've been really worried.'

'Well, still alive. And I'm still going to publish. I'm damned if I'll let some cowardly anonymous letter put me off. I mean, how dare they? No signature, no explanation—just a death threat. It's outrageous!' Aidan sighed heavily. 'Sorry to rant, Sam, I think I've got over the shock and now I'm just—well, just plain angry.'

'I don't blame you. It's a horrible thing to happen. Tell me, when did it arrive, and what did it look like?'

'Oh, well now, it was at least a week ago: it must have been Saturday. Yes, it arrived on Saturday. I remember now, it really knocked me for six and if it had been a school day I would have ended up running late.'

'And what did it look like? I mean, were you a bit suspicious about it? I don't know about you, but I really don't get many letters through the post.'

'No, me neither, which made me wonder what it would be about. Most people call or message, so why a letter? Anyway, it was a bit non-descript: a cheap envelope, address written in capitals. Oh yes, I couldn't read the postmark because that was completely smudged.'

'And the letter?' prompted Sam.

'That was on A4 paper. You know, ruled paper with the holes so you can put it in a ring binder. The message was made up of print. I don't know, it could have been from a magazine or a book. Not a newspaper.'

'And it just had those words on it *kill the book or we kill you?*'

'Yep. I just sat and looked at it. It was horrible. Somehow I felt contaminated by it, by having it in the kitchen. Weird.'

'You didn't think about keeping it, and showing the police?'

'No, not really. I wanted to get rid of it. I screwed it up and stuffed it in the bin,' said Aidan. 'Then I got an email from Amy with the offer of a contract for a series to follow on from *Superswamp*. Normally, I'd jump at the chance, but this has really taken the shine off doing another book.'

'Yes, it would do,' said Sam. She and Aidan were quiet for a moment, Sam nibbling her bottom lip, deep in thought.

'Do you want to find out who sent it?' she asked, breaking the silence.

'Yes,' said Aidan tentatively. 'Yes … yes, I do. If only to find out *why*.'

'Right, let's try and think this through. Who knew about the book?'

'Loads of people. It wasn't a secret. I hadn't tried to keep it as a surprise until it was published. So, teachers and the kids at school, and no doubt some of the parents. My family. Friends. I didn't put it on Facebook though. I thought I'd wait until it was printed and I could flash the cover around!' Sam heard a fleeting grin in his voice.

'Anyone who would be desperate for you not to publish?'

'It's hard to imagine. I mean, what could they possibly have against it? Or me?' Aidan asked, with a worried note in his voice once again.

'The way the message was worded, it sounded as though they were more against the book than you. But if you got in the way and published it, they would deal with you.'

'No one's actually seen the book. I've told people the idea came out of the school trip. But they don't know the story, or the characters. Only you, Jen, and other staff at Phoenix Publishing have seen the story and Jen's illustrations. I don't know who the staff at Phoenix show it to,' Aidan said. 'I can't think of anyone who'd want to kill it.'

'I can't either,' said Sam. 'But I'll think on it. Do you want this kept quiet, or shall I let Charlotte know? The other person who might be really helpful on this is Nate. Remember, you met him last year at Phoenix's Christmas party. He used to be in the police force and he's got one of those brains that can come up different ways of looking at things.'

'I think you'll have to let Charlotte know. If it ever came out, she'd be annoyed about being kept in the dark. Oh God, and if anything happens to me, or to staff at Phoenix for publishing the book … oh no, it doesn't bear thinking about. Yes, tell her. I should have done it when I got the letter. I didn't think about any risk to the publishers, but there could be. Tell her I'm fine and not to worry about me.'

Sam nodded, thinking *he's not really fine at all. How can he be, with all this on his mind?* She made herself put a smile in her voice, saying brightly 'of course I'll tell her. You're right, she needs to know. She'll have to decide if she wants to go ahead with the book, although I can't see her pulling out because of one anonymous letter. It's such a shame because getting published is every writer's dream, and that horrible letter is casting a whopping great shadow over it all.'

'It is a bit,' said Aidan. 'And about Nate, yes, do tell him if you think he might have some ideas. Let me know how it all goes.'

'I will. I'm sorry I haven't been much help, but thanks for telling me.'

'It's helped to talk it through so thanks for listening. At least I haven't received any more threats, although I might do once the book is out.'

'We won't go there until we have to,' said Sam firmly. 'If you do get any more letters, I think you're going to have to involve the police.'

Aidan sighed. 'You're probably right. OK, thanks Sam. Speak soon.'

Sam sat for a moment. She wasn't sure how she felt. Part of her was very angry on Aidan's behalf, and a small part of her felt uneasy. Would anyone *really* kill Aidan for publishing the book? Were Jen and her colleagues at Phoenix in danger too? She sighed. *No point brooding on it. Glass of wine time.*

Sam closed the door of Charlotte's office behind her. She hadn't wanted to alarm her boss, but it had definitely been the right thing to tell her about Aidan's letter.

Charlotte's reaction had been mixed, and she'd told Sam how dismayed she felt that anyone would want to stop *Superswamp*'s publication. 'I can't see what possible threat it presents. It's a book for children. It's hardly contentious!' she'd said.

'It's nearly Easter, so the office will be empty for a few days. I'm not going away, so I think I'll pop in to check the post, and that everything is OK,' Charlotte said.

'Good idea. I'm going to look at the campervan my uncle has left me in his will, so I'll be away for a few days.'

'Please don't discuss it with anyone else. It's surprising how quickly word gets out, and I'd hate any of our other authors to get wind of this.'

'I suggested to Aidan that I ran it all past my partner, Nate. He's ex-police, and good at problem-solving. Is that OK? I might be clutching at straws, but Aidan is completely flummoxed and so am I.'

'Well, it's worth a try,' said Charlotte. 'But no one at Phoenix.'

'Of course not. No, we don't want to have a mass panic on our hands.' said Sam.

Sam hit the alarm button to turn it off, and stretched lazily. Easter had finally arrived, and she was more than ready for a break. It was cosy under the duvet, and she started to doze off again before remembering she'd arranged to be at her parents' house for eight.

Fortunately, she'd packed most of her things the night before, and she quickly showered and put the last few items she'd need for her short stay in her bag. In the kitchen, she put a few food items into some bags, just in case. It was an easy journey to her parents' house, but from there she'd have a longer drive to Uncle Harry's house where Hattie, the campervan, was currently kept.

The roads were quiet at this time of the morning. It would be a different story as the coach trips headed out to the Cotswolds' tourist hotspots. Fortunately, her route avoided these and she soon pulled up in front of her parents' house. The pale honey stone glowed in the Spring sunshine, and Sam paused to admire the display of tulips in the front garden. It was the house where she had grown up, and even though she had a place of her own now, it still felt like coming home.

The front door opened, and her father, David, stood smiling in the doorway.

'Hello, darling. Good drive?' he asked as he gave Sam a hug.

'Not bad. I'm glad it's a nice day.' said Sam.

'Here, let me take all that,' said her father, noticing Sam's bags. 'How long are you going for? You don't travel light, do you!' he said, jokingly.

'Oh, just for a couple of nights. But I thought we'd need a few bits of food for breakfast, and coffee and stuff. It all mounts up.'

'It certainly does! Well, come on through,' he said, leading the way through the hall. 'You'll learn the art of packing light when you're in the camper: it's got storage, but not a lot!'

'I can't wait to meet Hattie again. I'm assuming she'll be in a good enough state to sleep in overnight. If not, we'll have to find a b&b or sleep in Uncle Harry's house.'

'Hattie should be fine. Harry looked after her well. Better than he did his paperwork, that's for sure! Anyway, where's your mother got to? Elaine! Elaine! Sam's here.'

Sam heard her mother's muffled voice reply, and walking into the kitchen, she saw Elaine coming into the house through the conservatory, carrying some flowers she'd just cut from the garden.

'Hi, Mum,' said Sam, giving Elaine a hug and a kiss on the cheek. 'The tulips are looking lovely, and so are these. What are they?'

'Some rather late narcissi,' said her mother. 'I'll just pop them in some water, and we'll get coffee going. I assume you'd like one? Do say yes, your dad's dying to show you his latest bit of coffee-making gear.'

'In that case, how could I say no? Coffee would be great.' Sam sat down at the kitchen table, running her hand over the surface. How many meals had they eaten around this table? Hundreds, probably. It felt like the heart of the house, where the three of them ate, talked, and when she was growing up, argued. She reached towards the bowl that was always at the centre of the table, and took an apple.

David was already measuring out the coffee beans, and before long the smell of freshly ground coffee filled the kitchen.

'So what's the latest toy?' asked Sam, looking at the various gadgets on the worktop and munching her apple.

'This,' said David. 'The best thing ever for making coffee.'

'Oh, a Moka pot! They really are the best,' said Sam.

'Your father's decided it's the only way to make a decent cup of coffee, and I have to say, I do agree,' said her mother. 'The only problem is, we have to drink tea now when we're out as no other coffee comes close.'

'Oh dear, it's a tough life,' said Sam, amused. 'You never used to be such coffee enthusiasts.'

'No. This is what happens when you retire.'

'What, you drink coffee?'

'No, you have time to get fussy!' said her mother, laughing.

'If it means a good cup of coffee, I'm not complaining,' said Sam, looking at her parents fondly. 'So, Dad, what's the plan for today?'

'I'll drive us to Harry's place. You can have a look at Hattie and take her for a drive if you like. I've sorted the paperwork so it's all legal.'

'Great, thanks. You've remembered Nate's meeting us at Harry's?'

'Yes, I had remembered. I can drive home, and you can drive the camper back here, or Nate can drive you back in his car if you want to leave the camper at Harry's for now. I don't know if you've thought where you're going to keep the camper, long-term?'

'Hmm, I hadn't thought about that. There's not enough room really at my place, unless I sell the car, and I don't want to rush into doing that. I've never driven anything like Hattie before and I've got to make sure I like driving her. Nate said he'd help me. I hope he'll be patient with me though! Driving together doesn't always bring out the best in people.'

'You'll be fine,' said Elaine. 'You just need to get used to the size of it.'

'Says she who's never driven any bigger than a car!' said Sam, grinning at Elaine. 'But thanks for the vote of confidence!'

'You could keep Hattie here, if that would help,' said David. 'Obviously, Harry's place will be sold once we've got probate, and it would probably be better to have Hattie where we can give her a run out regularly, and we can make sure she doesn't get damp. Ah, that's the Moka working its magic. Just a few more minutes to wait for coffee perfection!'

'It smells wonderful,' said Sam. 'So, what other news is there?'

Elaine started to tell Sam about recent events in the village, as David finished making the coffee and putting the steaming cups, together with some shortbread biscuits, on the table. The conversation flowed easily, and the coffee and shortbread quickly disappeared.

'Now, if you two have finished nattering, shall we get going, Sam?' asked David.

The letterbox flicked open, and Aidan heard the post land on the doormat. He still felt a slight feeling of dread every time he got post, not that there was much. Today there were the usual flyers, and an envelope. Aidan's stomach flipped over. It was the same capital letters, the same cheap envelope. *Not again* he thought.

He perched shakily on a stool and turned the envelope over in his hands. Then, with a decisive rip, he tore open the envelope and took out the piece of cheap, A4 ruled paper he knew he was going to find inside.

Lips pursed, and with a frown of concentration, Aidan unfolded the paper to reveal the message. It was compiled in the same way as the last one, using words cut from a magazine or book. But this time it said:

REMEMBER
Kill the book or we kill you
Don't think you can get away

Aidan read the words a few times. He didn't feel as horrified as he had when he'd got the first message. He just felt sick, and disbelieving that anyone would send such a message. All he wanted to do was to hurl the paper into the bin, wash his hands, and forget about it. He sighed. He couldn't do that this time. He knew Sam and Jen were right, he should have kept the last message so he could show it to the police. He couldn't throw this latest one away.

He re-folded the piece of paper and put it back in the envelope, and put it between a few cookery books on the workshop. Out of sight, but not out of mind.

He should tell Sam, he thought. And Jen. He wondered briefly why only he had received these letters. He was relieved Jen, as the illustrator of the book, hadn't got any, but it was a bit mystifying. How did they know his address?

Aidan briefly messaged Sam, and then Jen. Almost immediately, Jen replied asking if he'd like to meet up for a coffee, or a drink later. He smiled. She was a good friend, and he'd be glad of her company.

It took Sam a little longer to reply. *Sorry for slow reply. On my way to view the camper and to meet up with Nate. I will get his take on all this, and update Charlotte on latest threat. Contact the police!! Stay safe. Will be in touch soon.*

He had every intention of staying safe. And of publishing his book. Whatever the outcome. In the meantime, he'd call the police. He sighed. This wasn't the restful Easter break he'd had in mind.

'Sorry, Dad, I need to give Charlotte a call,' said Sam.

'You're not working, are you? It's Easter!' said David.

'No, not really. Um, it might be better if we can find somewhere to stop. It'll just be one call, but something's come up and it's important.'

David glanced briefly at his daughter's face, before looking back at the road. She had that closed-off look he knew so well. He knew that pressing her in an attempt to find out more would not work.

'OK, we'll find somewhere for an early lunch, and we can put the car on charge while we eat. Is everything all right?'

'Nothing to worry about,' said Sam, feeling guilty that she couldn't be more honest. A few miles further on they pulled in to a service station, plugged in the car, and walked over to the café.

'I'll see you inside, Dad. Could you order me a tea and a sandwich? Anything will be fine,' asked Sam. 'I'll make the call out here to save everyone else from having to listen to me!'

'Good thinking,' said David, walking on the café. 'Don't be too long.'

Sam smiled to herself. She was still the child, even at forty-odd. As she scrolled through her contacts to find Charlotte's number, her smile faded and her face settled into a more worried expression.

The phone rang a couple of times before Charlotte answered, sounding rather breathless.

'Sam, is that you? Oh Sam, I've had one of those letters too. It's just horrible.'

Sam heard the distress in Charlotte's voice. 'No! Oh no, I'm so sorry. What did it say?'

'It's on similar lines to Aidan's.' There was a pause, as Charlotte swallowed hard. 'It says .... It says ... *If you publish any books by Aidan Wilcox you won't live another day.* Whoever sent it has cut out the letters to make up the message. That's what you said Aidan's letter was like, didn't you?'

'Yes, it was. And he's had another one today as well.'

'What? Oh no. This is getting serious. What did his say? Is he all right? Silly question really, but you know what I mean.'

Sam explained, hearing Charlotte's sharp intake of breath.

'That's awful. He hasn't thrown it away this time, has he?'

Sam quickly read Aidan's texts to Charlotte.

'Let's keep each other posted. Try to relax and enjoy your time away. I'm sure we'll all be fine, despite these silly threats.'

'I do hope so,' said Sam. 'I'll be in the office first thing Tuesday morning.'

'All sorted?' asked David as Sam settled herself at the table. 'I've ordered you a panini and a tea. OK?'

'Perfect,' said Sam, trying to look more at ease than she felt.

'Everything all right? You look a bit tense,' said David.

'No, I'm fine. Just need to get into holiday mode,' replied Sam. 'It's not always easy to switch off, much as I want to.'

'Well, we'll soon be at Harry's place. It's a bit off the beaten track, so I hope Nate won't have any problems finding it.'

'He's ex-police, Dad. I think he'll work it out. Oh, this looks good,' said Sam as their lunch arrived. 'Bon appetit!'

The car rolled unevenly from side to side over the rough road surface, and Sam was glad it was not much further to Harry's house. The sunlight filtered weakly through the still-bare branches of the trees as David parked the car outside a modest house, built of grey stone, with three windows at the top and one either side of the front door. A small garden, rather overgrown, extended down the side of the house, with a gravelled pathway where Harry always parked his campervan.

Sam stepped out of the car and looked around. It was all very familiar to her, from visits throughout her childhood. She almost expected Uncle Harry to appear from behind the campervan, hair dishevelled, with some tool or polishing cloth in his hand. But of course that wasn't going to happen. She sighed, and turned to look at the view that always drew her attention. The neat fields, edged with stone walls were laid out before her, stretching as far as the hills with their stonier slopes. Sheep grazed, their white fleeces standing out against the vivid greenness of the grass. It was an idyllic scene. *So English*, she thought, before remembering she was now in Wales.

'I've got the keys. Let's go inside and make sure everything is OK. It's been a few weeks since your mother and I came up to clear out the fridge. I'll make a cup of tea and then we'll have a look at Hattie.'

'OK. I'll get the milk out of the boot,' said Sam as her phone pinged. The message was from Nate. *Got a bit lost. ETA is 3.* Sam smiled. It would be good to see him, and Gustav.

Looking around the inside of Harry's house, Sam started to realise just how much her parents would have to sort out. While the rooms were quite tidy, any cupboard, shelf or drawer was stuffed full with books, papers, and knick-knacks from his travels.

'Gosh, he was quite a hoarder, wasn't he,' commented Sam. 'I don't think I'd really noticed before.'

'Yes. He lived here for much of his life and he didn't believe in throwing things away. There's a shed and a garage that's full of tools and bits of machinery. It's going to take some time to go through everything,' said David, looking a little worried at the prospect. 'We've got to get the house valued for probate, then sell it.'

'I'll do what I can to help,' said Sam. 'But come on, let's have a look at Hattie.'

As they went outside, Nate's car pulled into the driveway. David waved, and said to Sam 'I'll go and unlock Hattie while you two say your fond hellos.'

Nate got out the car and gave Sam a long hug. A reproving 'woof' made them break apart. 'Hang on, Gustav, I'm just saying hello to Sam. Let's get you out now.' Turning to Sam, he explained 'He's in a cage thing, and he's not really that keen on it. If he had his way he'd be in the passenger seat.'

'Or the driver's seat,' laughed Sam. 'Hey Gustav, it's been a while!'

Gustav leapt from the cage and out of the boot of the car, tail swishing vigorously and woofing happily, pushing his head into Sam's hand so she would make a fuss of him.

'What a welcome! Come and see your home for the next couple of nights! Dad's just opening Hattie up so we can have a look inside. Hopefully everything's in good order.'

Nate smiled at Sam's impatience. Clearly, anything more than a hug was going to have to wait. He followed Sam and Gustav around the side of the campervan. The side door was open, and David was already inside.

'Hello, Nate. Thought I heard you arrive. Good drive?' asked David, while shaking Nate's hand with a firm grasp.

'Not bad. I got a bit lost at one point, but I didn't go too seriously wrong. I'm sorry about Harry.'

'Thanks. It's a shame he didn't have longer, but he certainly made the most of life,' said David.

'Nice place, and a great view. How's the van looking?' asked Nate.

'I'm no expert, but she seems fine. Doesn't smell damp.' The three of them looked around the interior with its Dralon-covered seats and gingham-style curtains.

'Oh, it's rather homely, in a quaint sort of way,' said Sam.

'I think you'll be OK taking her out for a spin, and sleeping in her if you want,' said David. 'If not, as you said, Sam, there's the house, or a B&B.' said David. 'I'll get out, and you two can have a better look. Oh Gustav, I didn't say you could get in, but it looks as though you're going to give it your seal of approval,' laughed David, as Gustav snuffled his nose into the various corners of the camper, sneezing loudly and looking surprised.

'Serves you right, Gustav, for sticking your nose in,' said Nate. 'Well, he seems to like it. Shall we see if we all fit in, Sam? It's going to be a bit cosy!'

'Glad it's got an extension so we can open the roof when we're parked up. I don't fancy having to crouch all the time, and it'll be worse for you, Nate. Gustav! Well, make yourself at home!' exclaimed Sam as Gustav launched onto the seats and settled himself down as though he planned to stay there some time. 'He definitely approves!'

Nate smiled. 'I'm not sure how much sleep we'll get in here with Gustav, but he does look very much at home. We'll just have to make sure he doesn't claim all of our sleeping space!'

'I'm very fond of Gustav, as you know, but giving up my bed would be taking things too far. Oh, Nate, I'm so glad you're here,' said Sam, as Nate wrapped his arms around her. Just standing there in the warmth of his embrace, with Nate's strong arms around her made her feel safe and happy. She tipped her head up, inviting a kiss, which Nate was only too happy to give.

'Woof,' said Gustav, suggesting that it was time he had some attention too. His tail thumped against the seat cushions as Nate and Sam turned to make a fuss of him. It was easy to imagine that Gustav was smiling: with his tongue lolling, and eyes gleaming, he looked up happily at the two people he loved most.

'Are you going to take Hattie out for a spin while your Dad's here? You might want to have him next to you the first time you go out. I don't know much about campervans and your Dad might have picked up a few tips from Harry.'

'I'm feeling a bit nervous about it, I must admit. I'm a complete novice! Yes, let's talk to Dad and perhaps he can give us a run down on the do's and don'ts of driving her.'

Inside the house, David was organising the food to make a simple meal for later. He smiled as Sam and Nate came into the kitchen. 'Everything OK?' he asked.

'Fine. Gustav seems to love it. Nate wondered if you could talk us through any tips for driving Hattie. You could come out with me for my first drive, if you're feeling brave, that is,' said Sam, grinning.

'I don't know that much myself, but let's go and have a look. My life insurance is up to date so I'll live dangerously and take the risk, Sam.'

'Hey, I'm not that bad!'

'I know, just teasing,' said her father.

The three spent the next hour or so looking over the campervan, starting the engine, and getting a feel for the clutch. Eventually, Sam decided she could not delay driving it any longer. Nate headed off on a footpath that went across the fields, taking Gustav with him for a walk, while Sam and David settled into Hattie's front seats for her first outing since Harry last drove her.

'Ready for this?' asked Sam, checking her mirrors before finding reverse, and then easing off the hand brake. Hattie hopped rather inelegantly backwards. 'Oops, this is going to get a bit of getting used to.'

'Yes, she's not like a modern car. And reversing isn't the easiest first thing to do,' said David, gripping the side of the seat.

Sam eased the campervan round and turned onto the rutted road, nursing Hattie over the bumps. 'Hope I don't meet any other traffic,' said Sam.

'This comes out onto a bigger road in a minute. By bigger I mean it's two-way,' said David. 'You're doing fine.'

And she was. As the road got bendier, Sam realised how much harder it was driving without powered steering. Eventually the road widened out, and Sam soon learned not to flinch whenever another vehicle came towards her.

'There's a ruined castle along here, with a car park. Should be fairly quiet by now. You could try a bit of parking and reversing.'

'Good idea,' said Sam, sounding braver than she felt. The car park was emptying, and Sam drove cautiously to a quiet corner.

'Now pick a space and reverse into it. Remember, your mirrors are your friends.'

'Yeah, no reversing camera or warning beeps on Hattie. Just a loud clang if I get it wrong!'

'You won't get it wrong. I'll help you if you want, or I can just keep quiet and let you work it out.'

'I'll try it on my own, but if you think I'm doing anything wrong or I'm going to hit something, please tell me—ideally, before I actually hit something!'

'Tea or wine,' asked Nate.

'Well, I'm celebrating, so wine for me,' said Sam.

'I'd join you, but I'll be heading home soon,' said David. 'You did brilliantly, Sam. I'm proud of you.'

'I'm rather proud of myself—and Hattie. She chugged along very nicely, given her age and her inexperienced driver!'

'Did you enjoy it, in the end?' asked Nate.

'I did enjoy it, once I'd relaxed and realised I wasn't going to do anything that disastrous. Nothing happens very fast in Hattie, but then I think that's partly the point. You want to enjoy the journey as much as the destination, even if today's destination was to return here for the night,' said Sam.

'Here you go,' said Nate, handing her a glass of chilled wine. 'We can take her out again tomorrow, if you like.'

'Shall we get the bed set up for later? I meant to ask Dad how we did that but I forgot. Hopefully it's not too complicated,' said Sam, her arms full of duvets and pillows.

'Here, give me some of that stuff. Let's have a look. One thing we know, it won't be as simple as pressing a button!'

'No, Hattie is about as low-tech as you can get,' laughed Sam.

They found a light switch in the back of the camper, and Nate clambered inside looking for a latch or some way of lowering the back of the seats down to create the bed. Eventually he worked it out, and the bed was soon made up, ready for later. There was a space on the floor for Gustav, where they put his blanket, hoping he'd settle on it rather than trying to share their bed.

'Nate, there's something I want to talk to you about. Shall we go back into the house for a bit?'

'Sounds ominous,' said Nate, looking at Sam for a clue.

Glass in hand, and feet curled up on the sofa in Harry's sitting room, Sam sighed. 'It's to do with Aidan—you know, the new author who's written a fantasy book called *Superswamp*.'

'Oh,' said Nate, a hint of relief in his voice. 'Yes, you've mentioned him. What's up?'

'He's received two anonymous letters, telling him to *kill the book* or someone's going to kill him.

Nate winced. 'Nasty. Anonymous letters are so cowardly, but they really unnerve people—I suppose that's the point of them.'

'I was wondering … well, I was wondering if I talked it all through with you if you might have some thoughts on what's going on. Aidan's got no idea who could have sent the letters, and nor do Jen or I.'

'I'll try. I can listen, at least, even if I don't have a lightbulb moment.'

Sam gave him a small smile. Nate had proved his worth in a crisis before, when Kaye Butterworth, his near-neighbour, was killed in mysterious circumstances. 'Thanks. It's niggling me. I don't like to think of anyone wanting to harm Aidan, and now Charlotte's had a letter too. So I'm worrying about all of us at Phoenix.'

'I think you're going to have to involve the police.'

'I know. Aidan was going to contact them. But let me tell you what Aidan's told me about it all.'

It was past midnight by the time Sam and Nate settled down to sleep. Even Gustav was looking bleary-eyed, circling round on his blanket before curling himself up to sleep. It had not been the most romantic of evenings together, but Nate knew that Sam needed to talk through the threats Aidan and Charlotte had received. As he eased himself under the duvet, with Sam nestled next to him, his mind started to turn over everything she had told him. *Who was doing this?* he wondered. *And why? And how would they know that the book wasn't going to be published?* But his mind was too tired for any productive thinking, and he succumbed to sleep.

Waking with a start, he realised that it wasn't a troupe of drummers hammering on the roof, but the sound of rain. It sounded torrential, and didn't make him feel like getting out of bed. Gustav snorted in his sleep, Sam was snuffling gently, and Nate tried to return to sleep too, despite his mind immediately bringing back all the questions of the previous evening. It was no good. His sleep was over, and he gave in to thinking through the information Sam had shared with him.

It's unlikely to be family or friends, or anyone at the school. The book's no threat to any of them,' he reasoned. *So who is threatened by it?* That, he thought, was the key question. And suddenly, a thought came into his mind. *What about the place that had inspired the story in the first place?*

What was it called? Something Hall. Somewhere in Wales. But why would the book be a threat?

It was the only idea Nate could come up with. It didn't make much sense, but it was a possibility, and might be worth exploring. Turning over, he woke up Sam who looked at him in some confusion before remembering where she was.

'Ooooh,' she yawned. 'What's that noise?'

'It's raining. I don't think it's as bad as it sounds.'

'Woof,' said Gustav, looking around for the door.

'Oh no, he wants to go outside. And I need the loo too,' said Sam.

'Guess you draw the short straw then,' said Nate with a grin, claiming more of the duvet.

'You can go off some people, you know,' said Sam, finding her shoes and a fleece. 'Come on then Gustav, let's get this over with.'

'By the way, I've had a thought. About the stuff you told me last night.'

'Really?' exclaimed Sam. 'Oh, it's no good, you'll have to tell me when I get back.'

'Make it quick then,' said Nate from the depths of the duvet.

Sam slid open the door. Gustav jumped out, turning back as if to say 'what are you waiting for? *The rain to stop*, thought Sam, as she prepared to make a dash over to the house.

Sitting at the table in Harry's kitchen with her hands wrapped around a mug of steaming coffee, Sam watched Nate deftly flipping rashers of bacon in a blackened frying pan that had definitely cooked many a rasher in its time. Her stomach rumbled in anticipation of the promised bacon sandwiches. Gustav had not taken his eyes off the cooker, although there was plenty of food in his bowl.

'Here you go,' said Nate, layering bread and bacon and handing Sam her sandwich. 'Hope it's to madam's liking. No, it's not for you, Gustav. You can have a bit of mine in a minute.' Gustav looked at him, tongue out, with hopeful eyes and a gentle whine.

'Right, while you're munching your way through that, I'll tell you what I came up with—about Aidan's letter, I mean,' said Nate, as Sam looked at him quizzically while continuing to eat.

'There were two questions that were puzzling me: the obvious one, which is who feels threatened by the book, and another one which is how would the letter writer know if the book isn't published, apart from it not appearing in bookshops. I mean, how do they know that Aidan has 'killed the book'?'

'Mmm, good questions,' mumbled Sam, taking another bite of her sandwich.

'You'd already discounted the obvious people: friends, family, pupils and staff at Aidan's school. But the idea for the book, if I remember correctly, was the place where Aidan and the kids stayed for the school trip last year. I can't think why anyone there would feel threatened, but it's the only thing I can come up with.'

Sam looked at him, eyes wide with surprise. 'That's a genius idea!' she said before a piece of her sandwich went the wrong way. Once her coughing and spluttering had subsided, Sam sipped the glass of water Nate gave her. 'Aidan always said it was a weird place. It's where he got the idea for the setting of *Superswamp*, although it wasn't as weird as he's made it for the book. But how would they know about the book? And why would they feel threatened?'

'No idea, and that's the flaw, really. Where was this place? Somewhere in Wales, wasn't it?'

Sam looked thoughtful. 'Yes … it's called something Hall. Hang on—yes, that's it! Alwyn Hall. Hey, I wonder if it's near here?' she said, reaching for her phone to Google it. 'Here we are, Alwyn Hall, and it's in … hmm, I've no idea how to say the name. I'll look it up on Google Maps.'

Nate drank his coffee and waited while Sam checked. 'It's … it's about twenty miles from here,' she said. They looked at each other. 'Shall we …?' asked Sam tentatively.

'… go there?' finished Nate. Sam nodded. 'We could. We'd need to think up a reason for being there, if you want to get inside.'

'We can just say we're passing, and want to check it out as a possible place to stay for an upcoming school trip,' grinned Sam.

'OK. Do you want to go in Hattie?' asked Nate.

'Why not?'

'We'll need to unmake the bed,' Nate reminded her.

'Oh yes, I forgot about that. I've not got into the campervan way of life just yet! Oh no, that means going out in the rain again … oh well. I'll sort the bed out if you'll wash up?' asked Sam.

After a juddering start, Sam nursed Hattie out onto the narrow road once again. As she settled into driving the campervan again, Nate felt his shoulders relax and he could appreciate the beauty of the landscape, glimpsed through the small windows.

'It's great being higher up,' he commented. 'You can see over the top of the walls.'

'I hadn't noticed. Oh yes, you're right,' said Sam, risking a quick glance out of the side window.

'You're doing really well, you know,' said Nate, turning to look into the back of the van. 'I think Gustav's gone to sleep!'

'As long as you stay awake! How much further is it on this road?' asked Sam.

'You'll need to take a left. It's a bit further along here,' said Nate, looking at the map on his phone. Hattie's idea of a satnav was a road atlas in the side pocket of the passenger seat.

Following a steep and winding road, they eventually saw a sign for Alwyn Hall. 'I don't know how the coach driver managed to get up here with Aidan's school kids,' said Sam.

'It's not that bad. The coach probably found it easier than Hattie. She's not exactly built for hills,' grinned Nate, giving Hattie's dashboard an affectionate pat to soften any hint of criticism.

'Well, here we are. Gosh, it looks a bit—well, gothic!' said Sam. 'You can imagine all kinds of shenanigans here!'

'You've been reading too many ghost stories,' said Nate, with a grin. 'But I see what you mean. Look, there's even a tower! He peered out through the windscreen. 'It all looks a bit scruffy. Not exactly lively, is it. I suppose there aren't any kids staying here as it's the school holidays.'

Sam parked the campervan, and they both got out to look around. The front door was firmly closed and the windows gave no hint of anyone inside. Nate glanced up at the top floor. The windows looked blacked out.

'What do you want to do? Knock, or just have a look around?' asked Nate.

'I think we'll need to talk to someone to get more of a feel for the place. We can't tell if the letters came from here by just looking around,' said Sam.

'I'm just going to look round the other side of the tower,' said Nate.

'Watch out for the swamp,' said Sam, partly in jest, as Nate walked away, Gustav at his heels. She felt suddenly exposed, standing on her own near the front door. Should she knock, or wait for Nate to return? *Best to wait*, she thought. *Otherwise I'll have to explain why Nate's nosing around the grounds.'*

Elena knelt at the window sill, looking down into the gardens. Nothing had moved, nothing had changed. There were no children to cook for. Each day felt like at least three, with nothing to distract her.

I wish Cristina was here, she thought.

Who's that? thought Elena as a figure of a man, wearing jeans and a walking jacket, came into view. *Is there someone staying here after all?* The floorboards in the room above her creaked. Morgan would have seen the man too. She moved away from the window, disappointed there would be no opportunity now to make contact with the visitor.

Upstairs, Morgan cursed quietly. *Who the hell's that creeping around? We're closed! He's trespassing, and I'm not having that.* Morgan stepped out into the passageway and headed for the stairs. Reaching the front door, he tugged the door handle hard. The door flew open, and he saw a young woman standing on the gravel driveway.

'Who the hell are you?' he asked.

'Oh, hello, are you the manager here? Or the caretaker?' asked Sam, taking in Morgan's shabby jumper and pulled-back hair. She smiled. 'I'm Sam Holliday.'

'Er, yes, I run this place. I'm Morgan. You're not booked in, are you?' he asked.

'No, no,' said Sam. 'We were just passing and we thought we'd pop in to see if the place was as nice as it sounded on the website before booking it for our school.'

'We, you said? Somebody with you?' Morgan sniffed.

'Yes, my partner. And his dog.'

'Where are they, then?' asked Morgan, scowling as he looked around.

'Er, they're just having a quick look round. You don't mind, do you?'

'I do, as it happens. Oh, is this them? Hey you, you know you're trespassing?' Morgan called over to Nate and Gustav.

'Oh, sorry about that. All this gothic architecture looks so amazing, I couldn't resist seeing what was behind that tower,' said Nate. 'I'm Nate Braithwaite, and this is Gustav.' Gustav gave a low growl. 'OK, Gustav, no need for that.' He looped his fingers through Gustav's collar. 'He's friendly really.' Morgan sniffed. 'Any chance we could have a look round inside?'

Morgan looked uncertain.

'We won't take much of your time, Mr Morgan, but it would be such a help if we could have a look,' said Sam.

'Oh, all right. And it's just Morgan. I'll show you a dormitory, and the communal areas downstairs. I haven't got all day to hang around for people who turn up unexpected.' He held the door open so they could go in.

'Great, thanks,' said Nate, as he, Sam, and Gustav followed Morgan inside. Nate smoothed the raised hackles on the back of Gustav's neck, but Gustav was not reassured. *Interesting*, thought Nate.

Morgan showed them the dining room, and the outdoor clothing area before taking them up to the first floor and showing them a dormitory and staff bedroom. Everywhere had a closed-up look to it.

'What school did you say you were from?' asked Morgan, as they completed the tour. 'Just so as I know, if you book,' he added.

'West Langley,' said Sam, giving him the first name that popped into her head.

'That rings a bell. Didn't one of you lot stay here last year?' said Morgan, looking suspicious.

'Yes, one of the teachers from that visit suggested coming here again, but places can change so I thought I'd check it out before making a booking,' said Sam smoothly. 'He's an author now—the teacher I mean. He based his first book on the school residential trip, so Alwyn Hall will be famous!' said Sam, smiling at Morgan as she tried to gauge his reaction.

Morgan gave a small start. 'Oh, really? Hope we don't get hundreds of reporters outside the door, wanting to stay.' He grinned, showing his nicotine-stained teeth. 'Not all publicity is good news,' he said.

'You might get more bookings from schools because of it,' said Nate. Gustav gave another low growl.

'Nosy parkers, more like,' said Morgan, sniffing. 'You tell him to keep Alwyn Hall out of the news. Now, I've got things to do, so you need to be off,' he said, brushing away Sam and Nate's thanks and goodbyes. Gustav gave Morgan a baleful look, before trotting out to the campervan. With a woof, he leapt up into the van, settling down at the back as though with relief.

'Well, what did you make of that?' asked Nate. 'Gustav definitely didn't like the place, or Morgan. Can't say I cared for him much either.'

'I haven't seen Gustav behave like that with anyone,' said Sam. 'It's as though the place gave him the creeps. I can see why Aidan thought it would make a good setting for his book.'

'But are we any the wiser? Could the anonymous letters have come from here?' asked Nate.

'Hang on, let's get away from here. He's watching us out the window,' said Sam, reversing gingerly. Before she could drive onto the road, a white van turned in sharply, braking hard outside the entrance to the Hall, a shower of gravel rattling against Hattie's passenger door.

'What the …' said Nate.

'He's not hanging around! What's the big rush? If I'd been any further forward that would have been the end of Hattie!' said Sam, glaring at the van driver.

The van's passenger side door slid back, and a young woman stepped out. She glanced at the campervan as she pulled up the hood of her jacket. The front door opened abruptly, and Morgan stood in the doorway, gesturing to her to go inside. With a backward glance at Hattie, the woman went indoors. The van's engine was still running, and Sam decided to let it go back out onto the road ahead of her.

'I'd rather he was ahead of me on that narrow road,' Sam said. She waited, and then followed the white van out on to the road. It was soon well ahead of her.

'What an unpleasant man! He didn't like the idea of Alwyn Hall being famous, did he? And I was only joking, really.'

'Yes, but you said it to get a reaction, and it definitely wasn't something Morgan welcomed. He didn't want us there, either,' said Nate.

'But why? You'd think he'd want all the bookings he could get. It's a big place, and the running costs must be high.'

'I don't think anyone had stayed there for a while. I walked round the back and the gardens were really overgrown. It just looked … well, neglected.'

'So who was that woman? She didn't look like a visitor. And why would he need staff if it's empty?'

'I've no idea. He wanted to get her inside though, almost as though he didn't want to run any risk of her talking to us, or of us talking to her,' said Sam. 'Do you think the anonymous letters could come from Morgan?'

'I'm not sure, and I don't know how we could prove it either. All we can say is that Morgan does not want any publicity for Alwyn Hall from Aidan's book, and that gives us another question: why not?'

Sam sighed. 'Let's go back to Harry's and have some tea. My mind's a whirl and I can't think about it all while I'm driving Hattie.'

Easter was over already. The days had gone quickly, and suddenly it was time for Nate to return to Cumbria and Sam to drive Hattie to her parents' house.

'I'm glad I did so much driving with you. It doesn't feel quite so daunting having to get Hattie back to Mum and Dad's,' said Sam as she finished packing away the bedding. 'There, I think I've got the hang of that now. Are you up for another trip with Hattie some time?'

'Yes, if it's just a couple of nights. And ideally when the weather's good,' said Nate.

'Maybe the May bank holiday then, or I could take a few days off and come up to Cumbria.'

'That would be great. Come up before the tourists invade everywhere,' said Nate. 'We can get some walking in. Gustav would be up for that, wouldn't you, boy?' Gustav looked up, tail wagging at the mention of walking. 'I'll call you tonight,' he said, giving Sam a long kiss goodbye. 'Take it steady, driving back.'

'Yep, will do. Talk to you later,' said Sam, climbing up into the driver's seat. They'd locked up Harry's house once again, and as she looked back, a flood of memories came back to her from her childhood, and how much she'd loved her time with Uncle Harry. 'Come on, Hattie, it's you and me now,' she said, starting the engine.

It was a sedate journey to her parents' house, and uneventful. As Sam got more used to driving the campervan she found she could drive and think back over the weekend, turning over the questions about Alwyn Hall, the mysterious young woman, Morgan, and the letters. She was glad Nate had been with her. She had a momentary thought: how would her previous partner, Jack Henshaw, have behaved? She grimaced. He would have ridiculed everything about Hattie, and Sam's efforts to drive the campervan. He would have been rude to Morgan. And she would have spent the whole time trying not to annoy him. *Why did I stay with him so long?* she asked herself. She sighed. *No point going over all of that now* she thought. That relationship was over—finally. And now she'd found Nate. He was her rock. Not that she couldn't stand on her own two feet, but if the going got rough she knew he would always have her back.

Aidan picked up his phone, and scrolled through his news feed again. The anonymous letter was out of sight, but not out of mind. He'd thought of little else since breaking up for the school holidays. *Right, let's get this over with*, he thought. He'd found the number to call, but there always seemed to be something more urgent to do than actually call it. Like checking the news feed. *Do it!* He could almost hear Sam's voice—or was it Jen's? No matter, he couldn't face telling either of them that he'd still not got around to it.

His call was answered after a few rings, and he explained why he was calling. It was all quite straightforward. He simply needed to bring in the letter he'd kept, and complete some paperwork at the police station. And the chances of finding who'd sent it? Well, it was possible, but easier if he had some ideas who could be sending them. It was not entirely reassuring.

Maybe Nate's had some ideas, he thought, messaging Sam to ask her. She replied almost immediately saying she'd just returned home and would call later.

It was unlike Aidan to flick through endless TV channels, but he simply could not settle. Eventually the call from Sam came through.

'You went there—to Alwyn Hall? And did you meet the delightful Morgan?' asked Aidan.

'We did, and it was all really weird,' said Sam. 'Morgan clearly didn't want us there and it all felt so unused and secretive. I can see how it inspired *Superswamp*.'

'Sounds as though nothing's changed since Jen and I stayed there. Do you think Morgan could have written the letters?'

'He definitely wasn't keen on the idea that the book might trigger some interest in the place. Other than that, I really don't know.'

Aidan told her about making the call to the police.

'Good, well done. You might want to tell them they could have come from Alwyn Hall,' said Sam. 'We haven't got any other possibilities.'

'Yeah, I know. I don't hold out much hope though. The police won't have the resources to bother about an anonymous letter.'

'Maybe not. But don't forget Charlotte got a letter as well. I'll see if she reported it, and if not, we can take that in to the police next week as well. I don't know where we go from here though.'

'Well, I'm wondering about going back for a weekend—to Alwyn Hall. Maybe going with Jen. Would you want to come as well? Just to see how Morgan reacts. I do wonder about all the locked doors and the grounds being out of bounds. There was no maintenance going on, so maybe there was something else going on. Or is it a bit risky to go there?'

'It might be, but I do think we have to dig around there a bit more. Maybe Nate would come too, which means we'd have Gustav. He really didn't like Morgan at all—Gustav, I mean. He kept on growling at him and Gustav never does that. Would it be dangerous? I don't know. I mean, Morgan couldn't bump four of us off—five if you count Gustav … could he?'

'Look, all I'm saying is, they'll be even more of a nuisance if we don't take care of them,' said Carys as she folded her arms across her chest, hugging the tea towel to her. 'You've got to keep them happy, or you know what's going to happen.'

'But we don't need to mollycoddle them. What were you thinking of, letting them spend the day down here? Anyone could have come in.'

'And did anyone? Come in, I mean.'

'Well, no, but that's not the point,' said Morgan, reaching for his tobacco to roll a cigarette.

'You're not smoking one of those things in this kitchen, Rodric Morgan' said Carys, stabbing a finger at the offending tobacco pouch.

'Too right I'm not. A cigarette should be smoked in peace, and there's none of that with a house full of yapping women.' Morgan abruptly opened the door, slamming it shut behind him.

Carys shook her head, and returned to drying the dishes. *What harm had it done? They'd looked so miserable, and a day in the warm with some home cooking had perked them up. Perhaps they'd put in a word for Morgan to their uncle,* Carys thought.

Upstairs, the sisters settled into their usual places on the floor or the bed.

'That was almost enjoyable,' said Cristina.

'Yeah, Carys is OK. She's kind. Morgan's OK, but he wouldn't go out of his way to do anything nice for us. All he thinks about is keeping Uncle Marius happy,' said Elena.

'Not surprising, really,' said Cristina.

'Mm, true. Changing the subject, how did you get on—with the delivery, I mean,' asked Elena.

'Fine, I suppose. A long drive. I spent the whole day in the van. It was worse than being here. But we delivered everything, no problem,' said Cristina.

'Good. Uncle Marius is going to call tonight, so at least we can report everything's gone to plan,' said Elena.

'Of course you can take some time off, Sam. When were you thinking?' asked Charlotte.

'Probably the May bank holiday, so I wouldn't be out of the office for too long,' said Sam.

'Going somewhere nice? Are you heading off in the camper-van?' asked Charlotte.

'Yes, in the campervan, but I don't know if it's somewhere nice. I'm … well, I'm going to stay at Alwyn Hall.'

'Alwyn Hall? Isn't that where Aidan Wilcox stayed, the place *Superswamp* is based on? Why do you want to go there?'

'We've got a suspicion that the anonymous letters might come someone from there,' explained Sam.

'Nothing like walking into the lion's den! Sam, seriously, don't put yourself in danger. These letters are a matter for the police,' said Charlotte, sounding rather sharp.

'I know, but really, will the police take any action? They're under resourced and nothing has actually happened.'

'Nothing has actually happened *yet*,' said Charlotte, looking at Sam with some concern.

'And nothing will. I'm going with Nate, Jen, and Aidan. Safety in numbers: and we'll have a dog with us.'

Charlotte raised an eyebrow. 'Sounds like the Famous Five. Just don't expect all the loose ends to get neatly tied up.'

Sam laughed. 'I know. By the way, have you reported the letter you received?'

'Yes, I have. I'm taking it in to the police station later this week. And Aidan? Has he handed his in?'

'Same as you, he's doing it this week. OK, I'd better get on. I've loads to do after the Easter break,' said Sam.

As the door closed behind Sam, Charlotte sat back in her chair, hands behind her head to stretch out the tension in her neck. The last sixteen months had been stressful, with the revelation that her Publishing Director, Brendan McManners, had been planning to run down the company while secretly selling the popular *Granny Fi* children's book series to a Chinese publisher: a deal that had led to the author, Melissa Bingley, killing the books' illustrator who was also Charlotte's sister. *Gosh, what a tangled web that all was* thought Charlotte. From tangled web, Charlotte's new company, Phoenix Publishing was born. *Would I do the same, if I knew what I knew now?* she pondered. *If I hadn't, Sam and everyone else here would have lost their jobs. And we've got some great publishing, especially Aidan's book. No one is going to stop us publishing it. No one.*

Tea, she thought. *Keep calm, and drink tea.* She smiled to herself. *Drink gin sounds a lot better, but that'll have to wait,* she thought as she picked up her cup and headed out to the kitchen.

'We've got a booking for the May bank holiday.'

'What? From a school?'

'A group of teachers, I think. Wanting somewhere cheap to stay so they can do some walking, he said.'

'Right. With a bit of luck they won't be around much then.'

'I've put the details in the book. It's the only booking that week. We're busy after that, though, with the end of summer term bookings. Good thing too. We need the money.'

Checking the booking, Morgan noted it was for three nights for four people. 'Jen Somerville. That rings a bell.' There was a pause. 'You stupid cow, you've only booked in that woman who told you about that bloody book!'

'What book? What woman?' asked Carys, instinctively backing away from Morgan's pointing finger.

'The book that's set here! The woman who drew the pictures—you spoke to her, remember? You started all of this!'

'All what?' asked Carys. 'What are you on about?'

'All the …. Oh, forget it. I'm going out for a smoke.'

What was that about? wondered Carys as she went back to chopping the vegetables for supper. *So she drew some pictures for a book. Why was Morgan in such a mood about that?*

'Your problem: you sort it.'

'I've tried …'

'You are weak. You do not frighten him. I show you how to make him scared. Then I scare you.'

'No, no, no need for that. I'll sort it, Marius.'

'Yes. Do it. Or I do it. Maybe I kill him. You choose.'

Morgan looked at the blank screen on his phone. *When will this ever end,* he wondered.

The weeks between Easter and the first May bank holiday went quickly for Sam as she worked on the marketing plans for *Superswamp* and other books coming out later in the year. Some weekends she saw her parents as she called in to pick up the campervan for a weekend away. Having a B&B on wheels made it much easier to find somewhere to meet between the Cotswolds and Cumbria, which meant she was finally seeing a lot more of Nate.

Not long now until Alwyn Hall !!!! texted Sam to Nate.

Any more anonymous letters? asked Nate.

Not that I've heard replied Sam. *Maybe we got it wrong?*

Aidan looked around the empty classroom, shuffling a few chairs neatly under the tables. The school was empty of children, and he was ready to head home for the weekend.

'I'm going for a quick pint,' said Gavin from the doorway to Aidan's classroom. 'You up for one?'

'I would, but I've got a call with the publishers about the book so I need to get home. Next week, maybe?'

'Forgot you were about to be a famous author. Drinks will soon be on you then!' grinned Gavin.

'I'll buy you a pint when I get my hands on printed copies. In fact, I'll probably give them to everyone as an early Christmas present.'

Gavin grinned. 'It'll be good to see it. Anyway, I'm off. Enjoy your weekend.'

Aidan put on his coat and scooped up his things into his backpack, slinging it over his shoulder. He did a quick check, switching off lights and locking his classroom door before heading out of the main door to the playground. As he turned to go out the school gate, he thought he heard footsteps. He looked around, expecting to see the school caretaker or another teacher, but the playground seemed to be deserted. Suddenly, he was sprawling on the ground with his backpack thrown to one side. A knee pressed hard into his back and he felt a sharp blade at his neck. Instinctively, he wanted to struggle but forced himself to keep still.

'Do yourself a favour,' hissed a voice into his ear. 'Kill the book or next time I'll kill you. Got it?' said a voice close to his ear.

It was impossible to nod or shake his head with the blade so close to his skin. Aidan swallowed hard. 'Yes,' he croaked.

'You won't get another warning. Now, I'm letting you go. Don't move, and don't even think of calling the police. I know where to find you.'

Aidan felt the pressure of the man's knee slowly lifting. He shuffled slightly, and the knee was immediately pressed into the small of his back.

'I said, don't move.'

'OK,' said Aidan, his voice muffled by the sleeve of his coat.

The man waited a few seconds, then stood up and ran towards the gate. Aidan looked up. Trainers, joggers, sweatshirt with the hood up. Average height. Could be anyone. He'd stank of smoke. Probably why he wasn't running that fast. Aidan knew he could catch him, but he would be no match for a man with a knife. *What the hell was he going to do now?*

'Aidan? AIDAN? What the hell happened to you?' Gavin Davies was running across the playground. Aidan instinctively shrunk back. He'd got himself up onto his knees, but standing up felt beyond him.

'Hi Gavin,' he said, his voice sounding weak even to his own ears. 'Thought you'd be at the pub by now.'

'Forgot something, so came back on the off chance the school would still be open. Never mind all that now. Can you get up, if I help you?'

'I think so. I went down with a bit of a crash. Feeling a bit groggy,' said Aidan.

'Trip over your shoelaces?' asked Gavin.

'Tripped over by a man with a knife.'

'You're kidding me.'

'Nope. He came from behind me, knocked me over, and pressed the blade to my throat. Look,' said Aidan, pulling the neck of his sweater away. 'I bet it's left a red mark, or a graze.'

'Er, yes, you've got a few scratches. Nasty. Now then, I'm going to stand behind you and get my hands under your armpits to haul you to your feet. Yeah, I know, I don't want to put my hands in your armpits either but I think it's the best way. Ready?' Gavin manoeuvred into position, and between them Aidan was soon on his feet again.

'All right? Not going to keel over again?' asked Gavin, tentatively releasing his hands.

'No, don't think so. Do you still want to go back into the building?'

'It'll keep. First priority is calling the police, then getting you home, or to the minor injuries unit. In fact, why don't we go into school. Then you can sit down, and I'll make some tea. I don't think you're in a fit state to walk home. I can sort out a taxi.'

'Police? No, no, I don't want to make a fuss,' said Aidan, as he gingerly took a step forward. Gavin immediately took Aidan's arm to steady him.

'Come on, old man, let's go and find you a comfy chair,' said Gavin.

'Just wait 'til I get my walking stick,' said Aidan. 'I'll be a menace.'

'You're that already, mate. Right, here we go.'

Sitting in an easy chair in the staffroom, the kettle just coming up to the boil, Aidan took a mental check of how he was feeling. He would have bruises on his knees and in the small of his back, and his shoulder was throbbing, but he didn't think that he'd banged his head. He still felt quite shaky, and shock would set in soon. Nothing felt quite real, and he realised he wasn't really taking in what Gavin was doing.

'Right, I've called the police. They will call round to talk to you later today, if they have time. If not, they'll call you.'

Aidan looked at him in dismay.

'What? Don't look like that,' said Gavin. 'What happened to you was GBH! Or do I mean ABH? Anyway, it was an assault. A crime. People can't go around putting a knife at someone's throat. The police have to know.'

Aidan slumped in the chair, feeling helpless. His attacker had been very explicit about not telling the police, and now they were going to turn up at his house. And they were unlikely to be in plain clothes and an unmarked car, so anyone watching the house would know.

Gavin made the tea, oblivious to Aidan's worries, sweetening the tea with a generous amount of sugar.

'Good for shock,' said Gavin, grinning at Aidan's look of disgust as he took his first sip.

'If the sugar doesn't finish me off first,' said Aidan. 'But thanks.' He sat up a bit straighter. 'It was a good thing you came back.'

'The police said it would be advisable to get your injuries on record, which means you'll have to go to the minor injuries unit. The staff there will want to know what happened, and so do I!'

'It's a bit of a long story,' said Aidan.

'I'd expect nothing less from you,' said Gavin, grinning.

'No, but this attack is linked to two anonymous letters I've received.'

'What?' asked Gavin, eyebrows raised, and a look of disbelief on his face. 'What letters? You never said anything about those.'

'No, I didn't want to think about them. But this is what happened …'

The police had left, the nurse at the minor injuries unit had cleaned his grazes, and as he started to relax he felt a headache waiting to pounce. It had been a long evening, and Aidan wanted nothing more than to crawl under the duvet and sleep. The police had suggested he got CCTV installed but he couldn't think about that right now.

Checking his phone before heading for bed, he realised he'd

completely forgotten about the call with Amy and Sam at Phoenix Publishing. Amy had left a message, suggesting they rearranged for after the bank holiday. Sam had also messaged him a couple of times, sounding increasingly concerned. He quickly messaged them both to hold off any more enquiries, but he knew Sam would have to know what had happened. After all, he was going to Alwyn Hall with her, Nate, and Jen at the end of next week. *Should we go?* Aidan wondered. *Am I putting them in danger?* His brain refused to think about it as sleep took over.

The ringing was persistent. Was it in his head? No, the headache had gone. Of course, it was his phone. Aidan swung his legs round so his feet were on the floor. Everything ached. *I've aged about thirty years* thought Aidan, as he gingerly stood up. His knees were sore, and his shoulder ached.

'Hi Sam, sorry, I didn't get to the phone in time to take your call,' he said, trying to sound his usual self.

'Is everything all right? You sound a bit weary,' said Sam.

'I'm fine, but … well, let's say, there's been developments.'

'What do you mean? Another letter?'

'No, a visit in person this time. Someone jumped me as I was coming out of school yesterday.' He quickly explained what had happened.

'What? Are you sure you're all right? Did you see who it was?'

'Not really. Just a bloke in joggers and a hoodie. Could have been anyone. And before you ask, yes, the police know about it. Not that they can really do anything. They recommended getting CCTV installed in case he tries to get in here. I don't know what to do about going to Alwyn Hall next week. I don't want to put any of us in danger.'

'Hmm, well, they'll be four of us. I'm fed up with these threats —it's all so cowardly. Personally, I want to find out what's going on. Don't you?' said Sam.

'I do. I don't want to be looking over my shoulder, wondering when the next attack's going to happen. You're right, it's bullying and cowardly. I'll talk to Jen, if you want to talk to Nate to see how he feels. No hard feelings if anyone wants to pull out.'

'I think I should tell Charlotte as well. She needs to be on her guard,' said Sam. It was probably time to put the staff at Phoenix on the alert too.

Sam looked around the table at her colleagues. It brought back memories of the police briefings at the same table in the days of Little Bear publishing. She saw a few worried looks around the table as Charlotte entered the room.

'Good morning. Thanks for meeting me here. Don't look so worried! Everything's going to be fine. But I do have to brief you on a couple of things that are going on.' She settled into a seat, and taking a deep breath, she spoke carefully. 'As you know, we're publishing a book called *Superswamp—get me out* at Christmas. It's by a new author, Aidan Wilcox. Now for some reason, Aidan has received two anonymous letters, threatening him if he goes ahead and publishes. I've received a letter as well.' She paused to wait for the gasps and mutters of disbelief to quieten.

'The police are aware. But things have now escalated. On Friday, Aidan was attacked outside the school where he teaches, and ordered not to publish.'

There were gasps and a few exclamations of disbelief from around the table.

'Is he all right?' asked Amy, Aidan's editor.

'A bit shaken, but otherwise fine.'

'No wonder he's dithering about signing a new contract. And that must be why he missed our meeting on Friday,' said Amy.

'Are we under threat too?' asked Jason. 'Is that why you're telling us this?'

'I'm not sure if there's any threat to you,' said Charlotte. 'This person—or people—definitely don't want us to publish. The letter here was addressed to the Managing Director, not to a specific name. I think the threat is more likely to be to the business: to the premises. Something that would disrupt our work and stop us being able to publish.'

'Like a fire, or hacking into our computer system,' suggested Jason.

'Possibly. I don't want to make a big thing of this, but we do all need to look out for anything unusual. Be careful about emails with malicious links, or if you see anyone loitering around the building. We're going to lock the outer door so you'll only be able to enter and leave when Debbie opens it for you. You'll need to tell her if you're expecting any visitors, and you'll need to be at the door to meet them and to sign them in. If anyone asks why the door is locked—and they probably will—just say there's a problem with the door and we want to make sure no one gets stuck.' The entry to Phoenix Publishing was through a revolving door which had the potential to be problematic.

'What about the book? Are we going ahead with it or not? I suppose that's Aidan's decision …' Amy faltered.

'Both Aidan and I are determined that this book will not be stopped by bullying, threatening behaviour,' said Charlotte. 'The police are aware of what's happened, and we just need to vigilant. If you have any suspicions, let me know immediately, or if appropriate, call the police immediately. Now I realise this is all a bit of a shock. Go and make yourselves some tea or coffee, take a break, and then let's try to get back to work. I'll be in my office if anyone wants to talk. Sam, could I have a quick word, please?'

'Sam, are you sure you should go to Alwyn Hall? I don't like to think of you putting yourself at risk for a book,' said Charlotte.

'Thanks for that, Charlotte. But yes, I've spoken to Nate and we've decided to go ahead. So have Aidan and Jen. We think we'll be safe enough together, and we'll be careful. What about you? How are you feeling?'

'I'm a bit uneasy, if I'm honest. I'm also wondering what might happen over the bank holiday weekend. An empty building just feels like an invitation. I'm going to get the CCTV cameras set up. We've still got some from the last time this place was under threat, but I need to check they're working. I can get one of the team to help with that. Then I can just check the cameras on my phone over the weekend.'

'Good idea. I'd forgotten about the cameras until you mentioned them.' She had a sudden flashback to the time when Enid Price, who'd worked for the Publishing Director, had tried to take revenge on her boss, leaving threatening messages around the building. She'd used a knife to stick one of them to the wall in reception, and the police had set up CCTV, identifying Enid when she attempted to put up another threat.

'Stay in touch, won't you,' said Charlotte. 'This is getting quite nasty, and I really want to know you're safe.'

'What could possibly happen?' asked Sam, sounding braver than she felt.

As the kitchen area started to empty, Sam went to make herself a coffee.

'Hi, Sam. That was all a bit of a shock,' said Amy

'I'm sorry I couldn't tell you about it. Aidan didn't want a fuss, and Charlotte didn't want to worry everyone. Not after all the drama with Enid.'

'No, I get that,' said Amy. 'I'm worried Aidan might get cold feet though, and pull the book. There's a lot riding on *Superswamp*.'

Sam stirred her coffee. 'I know. I'll try to talk to him. We can't push him though. If anything did happen, the press would have a field day—and we'd all feel awful.'

'I know, it's tricky. I just hope it all blows over and we can get back to publishing,' said Amy.

May 2024

One big bag, or several small ones? Sam looked at the heap of walking gear, jeans, tops and bedding. She hadn't added towels yet, or her makeup bag. *How did Uncle Harry fit everything in? If I take this lot there won't be room for Nate or Gustav, let alone Nate and Gustav and their stuff!* Clearly, it wasn't possible to change clothes too often when you travelled in a campervan. One set of walking clothes, and one set of casual clothes would have to do. In a moment of ruthless determination, she put the other items away, and rolled up her clothes for the next few days into her backpack. The bedding would go in separately, as would her washbag and walking boots. It was oddly satisfying to take so little. Everything fitted easily into her car, and she headed off to her parents' house to pick up the campervan.

'You're an expert already,' said David, her father, approvingly. 'First lesson of travelling in a campervan: travel light!'

'Yes, a pity Uncle Harry didn't apply that to the house. I don't envy you sorting out all that stuff. Maybe we should tackle it together next month?'

'Good idea,' said David. 'Where are you off to this time?'

'Alwyn Hall, in Wales. Don't ask me the name of the village, I can't remember it, let alone pronounce it. I've got it on Google

Maps though, so I'll be fine. It's not that far from Uncle Harry's house. I could pop in and make sure it's OK—no leaking pipes or anything.'

'That would be great. It's not as if there are any neighbours to keep an eye on the place, so it would be good to check. Well, enjoy your weekend, and we'll see you on Monday evening.'

Nate packed his things for the long weekend on autopilot. As a travel writer, he was used to travelling light. Now all he had to think about was what Gustav would need: food, and bowls for food and water. And his lead, of course.

Downstairs, he checked he wasn't about to leave anything behind. His eye fell on the photo of himself with his wife, Jane. *Late wife*, he reminded himself, picking up the photo. The memory of their time together was bittersweet. If she'd lived, he'd probably be at home this weekend with her. But life took a different turn when Jane was killed on a police operation that went wrong. He hoped nothing was going to go wrong this weekend. He felt uneasy about Alwyn Hall, and uneasy about staying there. He knew he would hate anything to happen to Sam. *Safety in numbers*, he told himself, shouldering his backpack. A small voice in his head said *Didn't help with Jane though, did it?*

Aidan looked at the block where he kept his kitchen knives. *Don't be daft*, he thought. *Even if we do get to a point where we need to defend ourselves, carrying a knife isn't going to go well if the police get involved.*

He checked his bag, and on an impulse, added the set of spare proofs for *Superswamp*. *Might show them to Morgan. See if I get a reaction*, he thought.

Car loaded, it was a quick journey to Jen's, where she was waiting for him.

'Good grief, how long are you going for?' he asked, looking at the large bag, back pack, and multiple carrier bags.

'Er, just the long weekend, but I wasn't sure what I'd need or what the weather would be like. It'll all fit in, won't it? I've got my drawing stuff as well, just in case I feel inspired!'

Aidan grinned and said 'Luckily for you I've got my NVQ Level 3 in Packing Multiple Bags into Small Spaces.'

'Now you're just showing off,' said Jen, watching him as he assessed each bag before carefully stowing them into the boot. 'If I'd known, I would have brought more,' she teased.

'Oh no. This is your lot. Come on, let's get going, or we'll be late for meeting up with Nate and Sam. Harry's house is not that easy to find, apparently.'

'Well, luckily for you, I've got my NVQ Level 3 in navigating,' said Jen with a grin.

'I think that's called Google Maps, isn't it?'

'You can go off some people, you know,' said Jen, fastening her seat belt. 'Toffee bonbon?' she asked, holding out a slightly sticky paper bag to Aidan.

'What, no jellybeans?' teased Aidan.

'I don't actually like jellybeans. It's just something I say when I'm a bit shocked or surprised. My family were really strict about not swearing, and 'oh dear' really didn't do it for me. So I hit on 'jumping jellybeans.' It used to drive my dad mad, but he couldn't suggest anything better so it stuck. He even says it himself, sometimes.' She paused and prised a toffee bonbon out of the paper bag for herself. 'Mmm, these are good,' she said, chewing thoughtfully and falling quiet for a few minutes.

Aidan grinned at her. 'Keep eating the bonbons. It's nice to have some quiet.' Jen glared at him, unable to speak with a mouth full of chewy toffee.

'Who are these people? And why do they come now?' asked Cristina, standing in the doorway of the kitchen. Condensation streamed down the windows while pots of various sizes simmered on the Aga.

'I've told you,' said Morgan. 'Carys took the booking. They're teachers, staying here to do some walking. They'll be off out every day. You won't see them.'

'Tell them, just use eating rooms and bedrooms. Like last time. Oh, Uncle Marius arrives soon.' She smiled at Morgan's shocked face. 'What, you think he won't check this place—and you? Like your teachers check out this place? He will not like to see them here.'

Morgan pulled his hair back, tightening the ponytail, and hitching up his joggers. 'That's great, that is. He might have given some warning.'

'You have warning. I give warning now.'

'Well, everything's fine upstairs. We've done everything he's wanted. Can't see he's got that much to moan about.'

'You do not want to see my uncle angry,' said Cristina, giving a slight shudder. 'He is angry man.'

'Wish I'd never met him,' said Morgan. 'Where's Carys? I'd better tell her there might be an extra mouth to feed. I suppose you've not got any idea when Marius will get here?'

'When he wants,' said Cristina sweetly, closing the kitchen door gently behind her.

Marius waited while the customs official scanned his passport. He didn't expect there to be a problem, but he didn't trust officials. The passport was new. He had never left Romania before.

'Purpose of visit?' asked the customs officer.

'Holiday,' replied Marius.

'Where are you staying?'

'In Wales. I visit friends.'

'OK, you can go through,' said the official, handing Marius his stamped passport.

Marius let in the clutch and drove carefully onwards. He realised he's been holding his breath. But they had not searched his car, and they had not really questioned him. *They think they're so smart,* he thought. Looking at his satnav, he saw it was going to take him several hours to reach Alwyn Hall. He would still arrive much sooner than anyone there expected. He smiled to himself and relaxed. It always felt good to put others on edge.

'Here they are. They can't have got too lost!' said Sam, standing by the campervan. Aidan turned into the driveway, and Jen leapt out of the car as soon as it had stopped.

'Sam! Ooh, this is so exciting!' she exclaimed, hugging her friend. 'Hi Nate—and Gustav! We haven't met before. I'm Jen.'

'Well, I didn't think you were Aidan,' said Nate with a grin. 'I didn't have him down as a dungaree-wearing man,' he said, looking at Jen's usual attire of denim dungarees with colourful patches on the knees. 'Gustav, gently now, Jen's a friend,' he said as Gustav rushed towards Jen and Aidan, anxious to check out the new arrivals. After hugs and handshakes, Sam suggested they all had a quick coffee before heading off to Alwyn Hall.

'I just want to check the house and garden quickly. As you can see, there are no close neighbours to keep an eye on things.'

'It's really quite isolated, despite the road. We didn't see any other traffic. It's so peaceful here,' said Aidan, looking across to the hills.

'A great place for writing,' said Sam.

'Not so great if you're getting anonymous letters about your book. You'd feel very vulnerable,' said Aidan.

'How are you now?' asked Nate. 'No lasting damage after you were tackled to the ground?'

'No, just a bit jumpy if anyone gets too close—like in the supermarket,' said Aidan, rubbing his shoulder.

'Does the shoulder still hurt?' asked Sam.

'Just a bit. It's eased off, and everything else is fine. I was lucky it wasn't worse, really,' said Aidan.

'It doesn't bear thinking about,' said Sam with a shudder. 'Come on in, I'll sort out some coffee. I've got some biscuits somewhere,' said Sam, rummaging through a bag of foodstuff.

'Don't worry if you can't find them, Sam. I don't go anywhere without a good supply of things to nibble.'

'That would be great. I think I've buried the biscuits in one of these bags.' Coffee and snacks sorted, Sam said 'I think we'd better have a chat about how we want to play things at Alwyn Hall.'

'If Morgan asks why we're staying at the Hall, we're going to say we wanted a base for doing some walking. And we can also say we're interested in seeing how all the maintenance work he was telling us about has improved the site, before we bring the kids on another residential trip. We'll need to make sure we play the part, asking about activities, equipment, etc,' said Aidan.

'Morgan has met all of us before. He saw Sam and me quite recently, so he may well remember and wonder why we've come back,' said Nate to Aidan. 'Sam and I can say that we only had a chance for a quick look and have come back to get a better feel for it. Checking out the maintenance work is a good idea.'

'And don't forget our main reason for staying at Alwyn Hall is to have a few days' holiday, and to go walking,' said Aidan. 'Jen, are you going to let Morgan think you're a teacher as well?'

'No. I think it's best if I stuck with what I know, so if he asks me what I do I'll say I illustrate children's books,' said Jen. 'And I'm here to have a few days walking with my friends.'

'That might raise alarm bells with Morgan,' said Nate. 'I mean, if you tell him you illustrate books.'

'We need to do that though, don't we. It's like baiting a hook to see if he bites. Morgan seems to be suspicious of everyone, so he's bound to ask us questions. And if our answers mean he reacts, then we can think how we can probe a bit more. So far, all we know is that he isn't keen on people being around the place, and he didn't react well to the idea of Aidan's book giving Alwyn Hall a bit of free publicity,' said Sam. 'None of that amounts to a crime.'

'I know … but remember, whoever doesn't want my book published is serious enough to put a knife to my throat,' said Aidan.

'We need to stick together at all times,' said Nate. 'Did you have a mobile signal when you stayed there before?'

'Er … yes, yes we did. I remember now, I was quite surprised,' said Aidan.

'So we keep our phones with us at all times too,' said Nate.

'Anyone would think you'd been in the police force,' said Sam, smiling at Nate. 'And let's not forget Gustav. He really didn't like Morgan when he met him last time. He wouldn't stop growling at him. Morgan will have Gustav to answer to if he tries to attack any of us,' she said, patting Gustav's head as he butted up to her, enjoying the attention.

'Gosh,' said Jen. 'I'm starting to feel as though I'm on one of Enid Blyton's Famous Five adventures. You can call me … George,' Jen giggled.

'Jen, we're not in a children's story now. There's no guarantee this is going to end well. If Morgan is behind all these threats, it could get dangerous,' said Nate. He looked at Jen's crestfallen expression and said more gently 'Anyway, before we all get completely spooked, let's clear up here and get going.'

'Yeah, the sooner we get this over and done with, the better. Jen, I think it would be best if we followed Sam and Nate, as Sam's driven to Alwyn Hall from here before,' said Aidan. Jen nodded, picking up the mugs to wash them up.

'Come on, Gustav, let's get you back in the campervan.' Gustav's ears pricked up at the word 'campervan', his claws clicking on the tiled floor as he followed Sam out for the next part of the journey.

'Girls, I need you to help me make up the rooms for these people who are staying this weekend,' said Carys at breakfast. The sisters nodded.

'A room for Uncle Marius also,' said Cristina.

'Yes, I know. Morgan and I thought he could sleep in one of the tower bedrooms. No one will see him there, if he's careful,' said Carys.

'Any idea when he'll get here?' asked Morgan.

'No. He has not told us anything,' said Cristina.

'Tell me if he messages you. Right, I'm going to sort out a room in the tower and get some heating on. You two can make up the bed when I've finished,' said Morgan.

His phone picked up a UK network, and the messages came flooding in. Marius scrolled through the list, ignoring most before stopping at one from Constantin. Marius scowled. London! He had a long enough journey as it was without a detour into London. But he would have to do it. He'd read the message now, so he couldn't make the excuse that he hadn't seen it. Constantin would expect Marius to follow his instructions. Marius sighed and punched the address Constantin had given him into the satnav.

Sam swung the nose of the campervan through the gateway of Alwyn Hall, and parked where she had stopped before. There didn't seem to be any designated parking, although she knew she could rely on Morgan to tell her if she was in the wrong place. A few minutes later Aidan pulled up beside her.

'Interesting drive!' said Aidan. 'Glad the roads are quiet.'

'I know what you mean. At least we didn't meet any manic white van drivers today!'

'Oh … oh yes, the last time you were here. Careful …,' and Aidan nodded to the front door. 'Hello there, Morgan. Aidan Wilcox,' he said, holding out his hand. Morgan took the sagging roll-up out of his mouth to give a grudging 'good morning' and a brief handshake.

'Lovely day,' said Sam, looking around, appreciating the blue sky behind Alwyn Hall.

'Won't last. Bank holiday. If you can't see those hills, it's raining. And if you can see them, it'll be raining soon, said Morgan, sounding quite pleased at the thought. 'But you'll be out walking, I expect, whatever the weather.'

Sam thought she detected a hopeful note in Morgan's voice as he said this. 'I'm sure we will. After all, that's mainly why we're here. As well as thinking about how we'd plan a school trip here.'

'Can't seem to keep you lot away. No one else does all these recces. Nothing much has changed since last time. Same rules: keep to the floors and rooms for your use, and keep the kids out of the grounds.'

'Oh, still no zip line?' asked Aidan. Morgan shook his head. 'That's a shame. Any idea when it'll be fixed?'

'Nope. There's just me to keep everything going, and a zip line's not my priority at the moment.'

'Well, maybe we can get our stuff inside. Where are we sleeping?' asked Nate.

'Second floor. Up the stairs, turn right, and you've got the first rooms you come to. And I hope that mutt's house trained,' said Morgan, giving Gustav a stern look. Gustav growled, his hackles raised. 'Not very friendly, is he,' commented Morgan.

'He's usually very friendly. Probably just a bit unsettled, being in a new place. Gustav, say hello to Morgan,' said Nate. Gustav sniffed Morgan's trainers and gave a short bark, followed by a loud sneeze. 'Sorry about this, I can't think what's got in to him.'

'Never mind all that. Now, I've got things to do. I'll leave you to find your rooms,' said Morgan.

'Thanks, we'll get ourselves sorted out. Oh, do you remember Jen? She came here before. She's the illustrator for Aidan's book we told you about,' said Sam. Jen smiled, tentatively.

'Yes,' Jen said. 'Alwyn Hall really inspired me. It's great to be back.' Morgan looked at her, frowning.

'I said before, we don't want publicity here, so don't go making a big thing of linking this place with some book. Not everyone wants to be a celebrity,' said Morgan, with an attempt at a grin. Jen winced at the sight of Morgan's nicotine-yellowed teeth.

Bags in hand, Aidan led the way to their rooms on the first floor. 'I assume we've got a mix of single and multiple-occupancy rooms. I can't see there'll be a double room with ensuite,' joked Aidan as he went along the corridor opening doors.

'We'll be fine,' said Sam as they came to a room with several beds in it. 'It's only a couple of nights. And after sleeping in Hattie, it'll feel palatial,' said Sam. 'Gosh, they're warm rooms, aren't they. Strange, the radiators aren't on. I wouldn't have thought there was enough sunshine to make it this cosy.'

'I know,' said Aidan. 'I remember being surprised how warm it was first time I came here, although I was really grateful for that in January!' He walked over to the window, undid the sash and pulled down the upper section. 'Ouf, that's better. Fresh air!'

'What do you want to do once we've unpacked? Explore? Find a pub for a meal tonight?' asked Nate.

'Let's meet in the dining room. We can probably get a cup of tea from the kitchen. I'll show you the rooms that are open to us—that'll take all of a minute,' said Aidan. 'Unpacking won't take long either. I gave up last time: the chest of drawers are all so wobbly.'

'Here you go, choose your bed!' said Nate, putting his bag on the floor and closing the door behind him. He spread a blanket on the floor for Gustav.

'Not exactly a romantic weekend away, is it,' said Sam, looking around the rather spartan room with its four single beds and functional chest of drawers.

'Could be worse,' said Nate. 'It could have been bunk beds!' He grinned at Sam, and although she gave a small smile in return he knew her heart wasn't in it. 'Worried?' he asked, going over to draw her into a close hug.

'A bit. When you reminded us this wasn't all a story it just hit me that we've put ourselves in a potentially dangerous situation,' she said, looking up at him.

'We'll just have to be careful,' he said, his chin resting on the top of Sam's head. While it was comforting to be held so close, she had a feeling he didn't want her to see the worry on his face.

Aidan knocked on the hatch door of the kitchen. The dining room felt chilled and unwelcoming, but Aidan thought that was probably because it hadn't been used for a while. A voice from the kitchen called out something, and Aidan stood back as the hatch door opened. He smiled at the young woman, her head and shoulders framed in the hatch door.

'Hello, any chance of some tea? There's a few of us staying here for a few days.' He frowned at the puzzled expression on her face. 'Ah, yes, I remember you now. You don't speak English.' He mimicked drinking from a cup and she nodded. A few minutes later she came into the dining room with a tray that held mugs, tea bags and milk.

'I get kettle,' she said.

'Thanks,' said Aidan. As she left the room he commented ' Gosh, those are the most words I've heard her say.'

'What?' asked Sam.

'When I was here on the school trip, there were two young women working in the kitchen, and neither of them seemed to know any English. Carys must have taught them a few words, although it's been over a year since I first came here so I'm surprised they haven't learned more.'

'Perhaps they have, and the one you spoke to is just shy,' said Jen.

The young woman returned with a kettle. 'Thanks,' said Aidan. 'I'm Aidan. What's your name?'

The woman looked nervous and said 'Elena,' before turning quickly away, avoiding any further introductions.

'A woman of few words,' said Sam, as Elena closed the door behind her. 'I'm not sure what to make of her. She seemed a bit—well, scared. We're not that scary, are we?'

Back in the safety of the kitchen, Elena breathed a sigh of relief.

'What's the matter?' asked Cristina, stirring the pan of soup she'd just made.

'It's that teacher again,' said Elena as she busied herself, tidying away the tray and scooping up the utensils Cristina had used to make the soup. She started running the hot water tap to wash up. 'He's been here a couple of times. He's with that group—the ones we made up the beds for. He told me he's called Aidan and he asked me my name. So I told him.'

'That's OK. Don't worry about it. It would have looked weird if you hadn't said anything, especially if he recognised you from last time. He'd expect you to know some English by now.'

'True,' said Elena. 'Do you think … do you think he might help us?'

'I don't know,' said Cristina. 'Without our passports, we're really stuck. And how do we explain why we don't have them?'

'When Uncle Marius gets here, we have to get them back. We've been working here for over two years now. Surely that's long enough to repay him.'

'I agree with you, but will he think so?' said Cristina. 'And what do we do if he won't give them back?'

Mugs of tea now made, silence settled over the group of four. Gustav settled down, the rhythmic sound of his tongue cleaning his fur the only noise for a few minutes.

'So …,' started Aidan, just as Jen started to speak. 'Go on,' he said.

'Well, I brought some copies of the illustrations for *Superswamp*. I wondered if I might leave them spread out on the table? Or somehow make a point of showing Morgan?'

'I've got a full set of the proofs in the bag in my room. I could leave those out as well. Maybe leave them on my bed, or something,' said Aidan.

'What do we expect to happen?' asked Nate.

'I don't think we know. But I do think we expect *something* to happen,' said Sam.

'Right,' said Nate, thinking. 'How about leaving an illustration or two out on the table after breakfast, and Aidan leaving the proofs out in his room while we're out walking tomorrow. Then if Morgan goes looking, he's going to find them. We'll just have to wait to find out if there's any reaction or any repercussions. That's when it could get dangerous,' said Nate, looking round at them all.

'OK with that, everyone?' asked Aidan.

'We all agreed to come here,' said Sam. 'We'll be on our guard.'

'Agreed,' said Jen. Gustav suddenly sneezed. 'Jumping jelly-beans, Gustav, you made us jump!' said Jen, and everyone laughed nervously.

'Any thoughts on a pub for a meal tonight? We didn't have a chance to try any of them out the last time I was here,' said Aidan, inclining his head to the door to warn the others that someone was about to come in. 'Oh, hello again, Morgan,' continued Aidan. 'Just the person. Any recommendations for a pub where we could get a meal tonight?'

The group turned to look at Morgan. With his scuffed trainers, his joggers with sagging knees, and his sweatshirt, he looked an unlikely threat.

'A pub? Well, you could try The Blue Anchor. It's walkable from here. Head out right on the road and take the first left. Can't miss it. Everything all right in here?'

'Yes thanks. Elena's sorted some things out so we can make tea.'

'Elena, eh,' said Morgan. 'That's …. good.'

'Oh, Morgan, I just wondered as there's no one else staying, would you mind if I left some papers I'm working on in here? They're quite big, and I don't want to keep them rolled up for too long,' said Jen.

'Yeah, no problem. Some of your drawings, is it?' asked Morgan.

'That's right. Just some ideas I've been talking to Aidan about.'

'Whatever … I've got to get on. Enjoy your meal.'

Sam phoned the pub to book a table. It was a bank holiday weekend and she had no idea how busy it would be. Looking around the restaurant area, there were quite a few tables with a 'Reserved' notice on them, including theirs. The landlord had greeted them on arrival, taking their drinks order. A couple of locals sat at the bar, nursing their pints of beer. They looked up at the newcomers and gave a brief nod.

'You're fine with the dog,' the landlord said. 'As long as he's well behaved.'

'He won't be any trouble,' said Nate. Gustav sat down, and arranged his paws tidily, showing just how well behaved he could be. Nate patted his head approvingly.

'Here on holiday?' asked the landlord as he sorted out drinks for Sam and others. 'Lovely day today, wasn't it. Forecast is looking good for the whole weekend, if you can believe that on a bank holiday.'

'Yes, we're staying at Alwyn Hall for a few nights.'

'Really? What's it like there? Is Morgan still there? He used to be a regular but he hasn't been in for—well, months. A year, maybe. Still alive, is he?' the landlord asked as he placed two glasses of wine on the bar for Sam and Jen.

'Oh yes, still alive. Not sure he's very happy about it though,' said Aidan, jokingly.

'Oh? He's all right, is Morgan. Works hard, and he always used to help out around the community here. But he's gone to ground recently.'

'There's only him and his sister—and a couple of girls—at Alwyn Hall. I think he finds it a bit much. He says there's a lot of maintenance going on, but it's hard to tell what he's doing.'

'It's a big old place to keep running. Didn't know there were a couple of girls working there. Local, are they?'

'No, they don't seem to speak much English. To be honest, it's a bit of a weird place. I stayed there a while ago with a school trip. It inspired me though: I made Alwyn Hall the setting for my new book,' said Aidan, looking carefully at the landlord to gauge any reaction.

'Oh, famous author, are you?' asked the landlord, finishing pulling the second pint of Felinfoel beer.

'Not yet. The book's not out until Christmas. But it might put Alwyn Hall on the map.'

'Well, let's hope it sends a few more customers our way then. Right, is that everything? I'll start a tab, shall I? Bethan will show you to your table.' He smiled and turned away to greet another group of people who were just arriving.

Aidan picked up the two beers, handing one to Nate. 'Cheers.'

'Well,' said Aidan, once they were all settled into the lightly padded dining chairs. 'No reaction from the landlord about Alwyn Hall being in the book.' He shared the landlord's impression of Morgan.

'I wonder if something's happened, or whether all the work of running the place has got on top of him. Maybe he's not well? He doesn't look healthy, but then he's quite a smoker,' said Sam.

'Who knows?' said Jen. 'I don't know about anyone else, but I'm hungry. What are you all having? I'm going for the locally sourced lamb shank.'

'Sounds good,' said Nate. Nothing more was said as they pondered the menu, tantalising their tastebuds with the prospect of delicious-sounding food.

'Jeez, if I hear anything more about this book, I'm going to … I'm going to …' Morgan spluttered to a stop, his hands clenched and face reddening.

'What? What are you going to do? Go on like this and you're going to have a heart attack,' said Carys, looking at her brother as he paced the kitchen floor, running his hands over his hair. He paused to pick up his tobacco pouch. 'What's got into you?'

'It's this lot staying with us—again. How many times do you need to check out a place for a school trip? And they keep on talking about this book—the one that's based on this place. And we've got Marius arriving any minute.' He stopped, and threw himself into one of the chairs at the kitchen table. 'What are we going to do?' he asked, putting his head in his hands. 'I'm never going to get out of this mess.'

Carys sighed, and put a hand gently on his shoulder. 'We'll be fine. The teachers will be out walking, and we'll just have to keep Marius busy. Maybe he'll want to go out with his nieces.'

'I don't think he's coming here for a holiday,' said Morgan. 'But yes, you're right, we've just got to do the best we can. I'm sorry, Carys. I know I'm a pain. I wish I'd never been to Romania!'

'Me too,' said Carys. 'Oh, me too.'

Morgan sat at the table, lost in thought. 'Yes!' he exclaimed, getting up suddenly and making Carys jump. 'The drawings: that woman said she'd leave them on the table.'

'What drawings? What table?' asked Carys, puzzled by Morgan's sudden burst of energy.

'Tell you in a minute,' said Morgan, slamming the door as he went out to the dining room. The papers were where Jen had left them, spread out on the table. He turned them round the right way so he could have a good look. Alwyn Hall! It *was* Alwyn Hall. Maybe it looked a bit more sinister but the shape of the building, with the tower alongside it, was unmistakeable. The drawings weren't originals, just colour print outs. No point destroying them. *Pity*, he thought. *Marius will hit the roof when he sees these.*

Morgan stood, deep in thought, not sure what to do next. He pulled his phone out of his pocket and quickly photographed the drawings. Another thought popped into his head: *what if Aidan had brought the book with him?*

As soon as the thought entered his head he knew he had to find out. Upstairs, he looked into each room until he found the one that Aidan was using. Aidan's bag was on the bed, with very little unpacked. Morgan unzipped it, and felt around the layers of clothing. Down the side of the bag was a wad of paper, which he pulled out and unfolded. *Superswamp—get us out!* leapt out at him from the cover page. The drawing of Alwyn Hall, with an area next to it that hinted at a murky, mysterious swamp, provided the cover illustration that he'd looked at downstairs.

The papers were proofs of the complete book, each page laid out ready for printing. It meant the pages were in a strange order, but as he looked more carefully, he found the back showing the blurb and more drawings. 'Inspired by a school trip to Alwyn Hall, Wales,' he read. It was in small print, beneath the waffle about the story. Again, he took out his phone and photographed the back cover. And then his legs buckled.

Morgan sat on the floor, clutching the proofs. *Marius will kill me for this*, he thought. He suddenly felt very sick, the sudden surge of bile making him cough. *I'm a dead man, even if I do kill the book.* He took another look at the proofs and tried to fold them up to fit them back in the bag. His hands, clammy now with a cold sweat, made it difficult to handle the paper, but eventually he got them back in. Standing, his legs still felt wobbly, but he had to get out. Back to the kitchen. To Carys, to safety.

'I think we need to do a bit of a recce around Alwyn Hall,' said Jen, resting her knife and fork on her empty plate. 'Oh, that lamb was so good. I know I'll feel guilty whenever I see one in the fields, but that was delicious.'

'Yes, good food all round. A recce, yes. But when? We don't want Morgan catching us,' said Sam.

'It'll have to be either late tonight, or early in the morning. Maybe look around the other rooms in the hall when we get back? I don't want to fall into that mud like one of the school kids, so perhaps we could leave the grounds until early morning.' said Aidan.

'Divide and conquer?' suggested Nate. 'You and Jen look at the grounds, and Sam and I'll check out the hall?'

'OK, let's do it,' said Sam, finishing her wine. 'I feel ready for anything after that meal.'

Back at Alwyn Hall, Sam felt rather less brave. Aidan and Jen had gone to their rooms. Having settled Gustav on his blanket, Sam and Nate went out into the corridor once again, working their way along it and checking each door as they went. The rooms were all bedrooms, sleeping 4-6 people, and were simply furnished.

'There's another floor,' said Nate. 'Shall we go up?' he asked Sam, talking in a low voice. She nodded. They walked softly up the stairs and opened the door onto the top floor corridor.

'I thought it might be locked,' whispered Nate.

'Why would it be?' said Sam.

'To stop children wandering up here?'

As the door opened, a wave of warm air hit them and within minutes their faces were running with perspiration. Again, they checked the doors on either side of the corridor but they were all locked. Nate looked enquiringly at Sam, as if to say *what now?* Sam shrugged her shoulders, then knelt down so she could put her eye to the keyhole of the door nearest to her. The room was brightly lit, and seemed to be some kind of greenhouse with leafy plants flourishing. With her face so close to the keyhole she could smell the plants: they smelt like citrus fruits.

'See anything?' asked Nate.

'Have a look for yourself,' said Sam. 'And see if you can smell anything.'

Nate gave her a curious look and knelt down to look into the room. 'Bloody hell!' he exclaimed.

'What?' asked Sam.

Nate turned, and she saw the look of shock on his face.

'What? Tell me!'

Nate stood up and whispered quietly close to her ear. 'It's a cannabis farm.'

'No!' Sam looked at him to see if he was teasing her but Nate nodded. 'Are you sure?'

'Yes. Well, it all adds up. The heating, the smell, the shape of the leaves on all those plants. There must be a fortune growing in there. Right above where the schoolkids sleep!'

'Let me have another look,' said Sam. Peering through the

keyhole she said 'I think you're right. Not that I'm an expert on growing cannabis, but I've seen photos!'

'We'd better get back to our rooms. I don't want Morgan catching us up here,' said Nate, pulling Sam to her feet and keeping hold of her hand along the corridor. 'Be quick but quiet,' he instructed.

Back in their room, they sat on Sam's bed, shaking with relief that they had not been discovered. Gustav got up, pushing his head into Nate's hand for a pat. Nate patted him absent-mindedly until Gustav started to sniff his hand. Suddenly, Gustav gave a loud sneeze, making Sam and Nate jump.

'Perhaps he can smell the—you know what,' said Sam.

'Maybe,' said Nate. 'What do you think, Gustav? I hope you're not going to get high on weed.'

'It's no joke!' protested Sam. 'We'd better tell Aidan and Jen about what we've found.'

'I'll message them,' said Nate. 'Go on, Gustav, back to your blanket.'

Within minutes there was a quiet knock on their door. Nate opened it to find Aidan and Jen, their faces pale with shock.

'You weren't the only ones to find something this evening,' said Aidan.

'What's up?' asked Sam.

'I got back to my room to find Morgan's phone on my bed.'

'You'd better come in,' said Nate, opening the door wider.

'What happened?' asked Sam, as Jen and Aidan perched on the edge of Nate's bed.

'After we said goodnight to you, Jen went to her room and I went to mine. My bag was on the bed where I'd left it. I hadn't unpacked much—I hate these chest of drawers—so I was rummaging through the bag to find my wash stuff. I'd pushed the proofs for *Superswamp* down the side of the bag, but I had this funny feeling that they'd been taken out. They didn't feel as neatly folded somehow. So I took them out to check, and moved my bag to spread out the pages on my bed. Morgan's phone was tucked under the bag.'

'How do you know it was Morgan's?' asked Sam.

'I didn't at first. I knocked on Jen's door to ask her if it was hers. It didn't seem very likely, but I was in denial, I think. It was horrible to think of someone being in my room, looking through my stuff.'

'We did talk about leaving the proofs somewhere in your room where they'd be easy to find, just in case Morgan did any poking around,' said Nate.

'I know. But I hadn't set that up, so I hadn't thought of it happening just yet,' said Aidan.

'I could see that whoever owned the phone had got one of those join-the-dot patterns to unlock it. Their fingers were really greasy, so it was easy to see the pattern. It was a letter 'M'.'

'Yeah, so we traced the letter M and the phone unlocked. Then we weren't sure what to do, but we decided to look in the contacts and saw Carys's name listed. A message came in from someone called Marius saying he'd be arriving soon. When we looked into his WhatsApp messages. There were a lot from Marius, with questions about Elena and Cristina, and about crops. Didn't make much sense. Look, I'll show you,' said Aidan, handing the phone to Nate and Sam.

The two looked at the screen as Nate scrolled through the messages and contacts.

'It has to be Morgan's,' agreed Nate. 'Do you think he took any photos of the proofs?'

'Have a look,' said Aidan. Nate opened up Morgan's photo gallery, and there were the last images he'd taken. He showed them to the others. 'I'd say that proves he's a bit obsessed with the book.' There were nods of agreement.

'The thing is, what the hell do we do now? I don't want him knowing that we know he's been in my room, or that we could have looked at his phone,' said Aidan.

'No, we don't want that,' said Sam. 'And there's more to tell you. You know we messaged you just now?'

'Oh yeah, sorry,' said Aidan.

'Did you discover something?' asked Jen.

'You could say that,' said Sam. 'It's just empty bedrooms on this floor. But the top floor? That's a whole different world. For a start, it's really, really warm.'

'OK,' said Aidan. 'Go on.'

'All the doors were locked, but we looked through the keyhole of one of them. There were bright lights on in the room—not like the pathetic bulbs everywhere else. These were really bright lights. And there was this smell, this citrusy smell,' said Sam.

'And when I looked, I could see a forest of cannabis plants. Like a cannabis farm,' finished Nate.

'What?' said Jen and Aidan together. 'Jumping jellybeans!' added Jen.

'Well,' said Aidan, 'that does make sense …'

'It explains why we've got limited access, why Morgan's so twitchy, and why our rooms are so warm.' said Jen.

'How can he do this? It's an activity centre for children, for pity's sake. Growing cannabis above children's heads? That's sick,' said Aidan.

'It has to be Morgan. There's no way that stuff could be growing up there without him knowing about it,' said Sam. 'And it does explain the references to crops in his WhatsApp messages.'

'Of course he knows,' said Aidan. 'That's why he doesn't want anything drawing attention to Alwyn Hall: it's a bloody cannabis farm!'

'Keep your voice down,' said Nate. 'I know how angry you are, but we don't want to let on to Morgan that we know. That stuff's worth a fortune, and whoever's running this venture isn't going to take kindly to us poking our noses in.'

'We need to involve the police,' said Jen, looking at the others. 'Don't we?'

'We do, but personally, I'd like to find out more about this whole enterprise first. Do you really think Morgan's got the wherewithal to grow that amount of weed, prepare it for sale on the streets, and organise a network of dealers? I think he's just a cog in a much larger wheel, perhaps working with this Marius person he keeps messaging,' said Nate.

'I agree with you, but how do we find out?' asked Aidan.

'We're here for two more nights. Let's see what else happens. We haven't checked out the grounds yet. And let's see if we get a chance to take any incriminating photos,' suggested Sam.

'What, of Morgan posing proudly next to his prize cannabis plant?' asked Jen, grinning. Nate gave her a withering look. 'Only kidding,' said Jen hastily.

'I need to get rid of this phone,' said Aidan. 'Any ideas?'

'I know,' said Jen. Nate looked at her warily. 'No, really, this is a good idea,' she said. 'There's a table in the hallway. What about putting it under there, as though it had dropped on the floor and got kicked under it?'

'That's not a bad idea,' said Nate. 'What do you think, Aidan?'

'I think it's a good idea. I'll go down, and if I run into Morgan I'll just say I'm popping out to get something out of the car.'

'Right, go for it. If you're not back in five minutes we'll be coming to look for you,' said Nate.

'Thanks, guys,' said Aidan, pushing Morgan's phone into the side pocket of his trousers. 'Let's get this over and done with.'

Sam's phone pinged, just as she was about to get ready for bed. 'It's Aidan. He says 'mission accomplished' so Morgan's phone is now in place. Gosh, it's past midnight! And we'll have to be up early to go walking, otherwise Morgan will get suspicious.'

'Let's get some sleep then,' said Nate, wriggling under his duvet. 'These beds have seen better days. Mine sags in the middle, and it creaks!' he said, demonstrating.

'Mine's the same,' said Sam. 'Not made for a romantic getaway, are they. Never mind, maybe next weekend.' She yawned. 'I'm shattered.'

Nate leant across the gap between the two beds, reaching over to kiss her goodnight. 'Sorry, that's the best I can do,' he said.

Sam's breathing soon steadied as she fell into a deep sleep, while Nate fidgeted, trying to get comfortable in the narrow bed. His mind was on a loop, replaying the heat of the corridor and the keyhole view of the cannabis plants. Morgan must have got the upstairs well set up to have such a flourishing crop of plants, which meant there must be others involved in drying the leaves and preparing them for sale on the streets. Getting more information wasn't going to be easy. Cannabis meant money, and no one was going to give that up willingly.

Morgan finished his last cigarette of the day, and went back in to the kitchen.

'Any news from Marius? Do you know when he'll get here?' asked Carys.

'I haven't checked my phone for a bit,' said Morgan. 'Hang on, where is it? I thought I put it in my back pocket.'

'Can't see it here,' said Carys. The table and worksurfaces were fairly clear so it didn't take long to realise the phone wasn't in the kitchen. 'I'll try ringing it from mine.' There was a very faint ring tone. Morgan stepped into the hallway and the ringing got louder.

'Got it. Must have dropped it on the floor. Strange I didn't hear it fall though.' Returning to the kitchen Morgan said 'I've seen the book—the one with this place in it. Look, I took a few pictures.'

'Where did you find it? You haven't been going through their bags, have you?'

'No, no, nothing like that. But look, it says on the back of the book that it was inspired by Alwyn Hall. And look at the drawings. OK, it looks a bit spookier than in real life but it's definitely recognisable as this place. Marius is going to be furious. I don't know what to do.' He handed his phone over to Carys so she could look at the photos.

'See what you mean. But what can Marius do about it?'

'Make my life hell, for a start.'

'Is there a message from him'? asked Carys, handing back the phone.

'Er …. Yes. He's arriving soon. What the hell does 'soon' mean?'

'Ask him.'

'OK.' Morgan sent the message and he got an immediate reply. *Tomorrow morning.* 'Great,' said Morgan 'That's all I need. Let's hope the so-called walkers keep out of the way. But he's going to want to know about the book. And when he does, he'll realise who wrote it.'

'Sure about that?' asked Carys. Morgan's withering look said it all.

Jen pulled back the thin curtain and looked out over to the hills. It was a perfect day for walking. Then she remembered last night's discoveries. *Not much we can do today* she thought. *Is there?*

Heading down the stairs, she could smell bacon frying. Going in, she saw her drawings were still laid out on the table, but not quite as she'd left them. She knew from the photos on Morgan's phone that he'd looked through them. As the other three trooped in, Jen knocked on the hatch door to let Carys know they were ready to eat.

'What's the plan for today, Aidan?' asked Nate. Aidan looked at him in surprise. 'The walk?'

'Oh yes, the walk. Well, I thought if you were all up for it we could walk from here, and do a circular route, going over the hills we can see from the window. I've looked at it on the map. It's around 10 miles, but we don't need to rush.'

'Ten miles?' squeaked Jen. 'Jumping jellybeans, that's more than I walk in a month!'

'You'll be fine, Jen,' said Sam. 'We'll take it steady, and you'll be enjoying the views too much to worry about the distance. Anyway, you can chill out when we get back, and you can tuck into a sticky toffee pudding later without feeling guilty!'

'True. OK, let's go for it. After breakfast—gosh, this looks good!' said Jen, as Carys passed plates of bacon and eggs through the hatch, followed by racks of toast.

'Help yourself to tea and coffee. I've put milk out,' said Carys. 'Just knock if you want any more toast.'

'No helpers today?' asked Aidan.

'Oh, you mean the girls. No, they're busy doing jobs for Morgan. Off walking today, are you?'

'Yes, we'll get going after breakfast so you won't see us for most of today.'

'Make the most of the weather. It might rain tomorrow!' said Carys, closing the hatch. 'Did you hear that, Morgan? They're off walking for the day. So we can get Marius set up in the tower room without him meeting them.'

Morgan grunted, and picked up the keys to the tower. 'If he turns up, send him over to the tower. I'll be working in there this morning.'

His eyes felt gritty, and he hadn't passed a café for a long time. The lack of caffeine was getting to him. London had been a nightmare: a warren of streets, and then he hadn't been able to find the address he'd been instructed to go to. Eventually he found it, and he finally loaded the boxes for Alwyn Hall in the boot. The spare tyre had long gone, and the space was used for more lucrative items. He smiled to himself. Despite all the hassle of the detour to London, business was going well and he was better off than he'd ever been in his life. And he wasn't going to lose that because Morgan didn't know how to deal with troublemakers.

Looking at the satnav, he saw he still had a long journey ahead of him. As the hours went by, the roads got narrower and hillier, until he saw the signs for Alwyn Hall. He pulled in to the drive, and parked next to a campervan.

As he went to knock on the door, it opened to reveal a short, thin woman with red cheeks, her greying hair pulled back into a ponytail. 'Hello, you must be Marius. I'm Carys Morgan, Morgan's sister,'

'Yes, hello. Is Morgan here?'

'He is. He's in the tower. Look,' she said, pointing, 'you can see it from here. We've set up a room for you in there. I'll take you over if you like,' Carys offered.

'Thank you, no, I go find Morgan,' said Marius, opening the boot of his car to take out his bag.

'I'll leave you to it,' said Carys. *Wouldn't want to pick a fight with him*, she thought. *No wonder Morgan's scared of him. And he didn't ask about his nieces.*

Upstairs, Elena was looking out of her window. 'He's here,' she said to her sister. Their eyes locked, and each knew how much they wanted to avoid seeing their uncle.

Marius strode over to the tower, carrying his bag as though it was empty. He tried the door, which was locked. He banged on it, and heard footsteps coming down the stairs.

'Morgan, my friend, here you are hiding,' said Marius, looking as friendly as a crocodile. 'How are things?'

'Hi Marius. Good journey?'

'Do not ask me about journey. Is terrible. Tell me about here.'

'All good. I'll show you round. Do you want to put your bag in your room?'

'You make good hotel receptionist,' said Marius, grinning. 'Where's the bar?'

'No bar,' said Morgan. 'But I've got some vodka in the kitchen back at the house. Right, this is your room, OK?'

'Is OK. We go now look at plants. I bring seeds for next ones,' said Marius. 'Why you not grow plants in here?'

Morgan sighed. 'Remember, the first lot went mouldy? You have to have a good air system to grow healthy plants. If you want to grow them in the tower, you'll need to pay for an air filtration system.'

'Maybe worth it. How many rooms here?'

'Eight rooms on four floors,' said Morgan. 'And all the water has to be carried up.'

'You are strong,' said Marius, punching Morgan's shoulder. 'Is good for you,' he said, laughing at the dejected look on Morgan's face.

'Come on, Jen, you're nearly there. It's amazing up here!' called Sam. Jen frowned. It had been a long climb for what felt like hours. She'd kept stopping and looking back at the view, which she had to admit was very lovely. But her legs felt like lead weights, and she was puffing like a Welsh dragon. *You can do this*, she said to herself. *If Sam can, you can, Jen Somerville.*

Staggering up the last section of the path, she gratefully took the hand Sam held out to her, and allowed herself to be pulled up on to the ridge. The path continued to the left or the right, undulating in both directions. Even at the top it wasn't flat, and there would be more inclines to walk up before the steep descent to return to Alwyn Hall. Gustav spotted her, and bounded up as though to congratulate her on having made it. He'd relished the walk, and had probably walked twice the distance, running off after an interesting scent before going back to Nate. Bending so she could put her hands on her knees, she could feel her heart pounding, and then starting to settle.

'Jumping jellybeans,' gasped Jen. 'That was quite a climb.' She looked out over the hills to the valley below. It really was beautiful. And as her heart stopped hammering and she could breathe more easily, she could see it was definitely worth the effort.

'See, told you it would be worth it!' grinned Sam. 'We thought we'd stop at the trig point and have something to eat. It's not that cold up here and we can enjoy the view for longer after all our efforts to get up here!'

'Good plan,' said Jen. 'Does that mean I can lie down for a couple of hours?'

Sam laughed, and said 'Come on, you'll feel better after something to eat.'

'So how high is this mountain? Not quite Everest, I know, but it must be close,' asked Jen.

'Er, it's just over 400 metres,' said Nate, checking the trig point. 'Snowdon's just over 1,000, so you'd have a bit further to go for Everest. But hey, you got up here. Everest can wait!'

'Ouf,' said Jen, sitting on a stone near the trig point. Sam handed her a box with homemade cakes. 'Wow, Brownies! You're a wonder, Sam. Thanks.' Gustav barked. 'No, not for you,' said Jen.

'Here you go, Gustav,' said Sam, offering him some dog treats. 'Good grief, I don't think you even tasted those!' Gustav looked at her, tongue out, grinning in the hope of more. The four were quiet as they ate and took in the view. 'Can we see Alwyn Hall from up here?' asked Jen.

Aidan looked at the map and pointed. 'Over there, somewhere,' he said. 'I could almost forget about it, up here. But I suppose we need to decide what we're going to do.'

'Well, two of us have seen the cannabis plants. And we've all seen the photos on Morgan's phone. I suppose he could make up some story about liking the drawings and taking the photos, but he'd have a harder time explaining what he was doing in your room and poking around in your bag, Aidan, let alone trying to explain the cannabis,' said Nate.

'We should report the cannabis plants. But I really want to get proof that he was the one behind the letters, and probably the attack on me,' said Aidan, absent-mindedly rubbing his shoulder that had taken the brunt of his fall.

'Ideally, we need photos of the plants, and something to link him with the letters and the attack. Or, we confront him about the plants and threaten him with the police if he doesn't tell us everything,' suggested Sam.

'The rooms where he grows the plants are locked though, aren't they?' said Jen.

'They are.' Nate paused. 'I haven't told you this, but in a former life I did learn how to pick a lock. The ones on those doors won't be difficult.'

'Hey, Nate, you dark horse! I'd forgotten you'd been in the police force,' said Aidan, grinning. 'We'd need to keep Morgan out of the way.'

'How about Jen or I keep him talking, while you and Aidan get into one of the rooms upstairs and take some photos?' said Sam.

'Probably easier to go up there when everyone else is sleeping,' said Nate. 'I'll try tonight. I'll be fine, Sam, don't worry,' he added, noticing her worried face.

'Are you sure about this?' asked Aidan, looking at the other three. They all nodded.

'Woof,' said Gustav.

Marius sat in the kitchen, trying not to look too disgusted at the coffee Carys had made for him. *This country!* thought Marius. *They cannot even make good coffee.* He took one of the Welsh cakes Carys had put out for him. The texture was unusual, but he quite liked them—enough to take a second one. Across the table were his nieces, Elena and Cristina.

'Everything goes well here,' said Marius with a smile that didn't reach his eyes. 'The boss is pleased,' he said, speaking to them in their native Romanian. He looked at his nieces to gauge their response.

'That's all very well,' replied Cristina, taking care to keep her voice neutral. 'But we can't stay here for ever. You said we had to work to pay off the cost of bringing us here from Romania. We have worked hard, and done everything you've asked of us. You say everything is going well. We have made sure it has,' she continued, trying to keep her voice firm. 'But now it's time to free us from this work. You promised us a wonderful future in this country. But here, we have no future.'

'You have a lot of opinions all of a sudden,' said Marius, slamming down his coffee mug. 'Who runs this business, eh? Do you keep the accounts? No, these are my jobs. *I* will tell you when you've paid off your debt.'

'We want our passports back. They are our property,' said Elena, keeping her eyes fixed on the table.

'Ha! You think I'm stupid? If I give you your passports you are free to go anywhere. No, everything is working well as it is. You will stay. Although I am sorry you have to drink such disgusting coffee. I am going back to the tower. I think we can grow more plants there, if Morgan works out how to control the heating.' He pushed back his chair and left.

'Don't say anything,' said Cristina in a low voice. 'He'll hear you. Let's go back to my room.'

Sitting on her bed, Cristina looked at her sister's rounded shoulders. 'I don't see how we're ever going to get out of this,' said Elena.

'We have to get our passports,' said Cristina. 'Perhaps he has them with him? If we can keep him away from his room, we can search his bags.'

Elena looked up, a glimmer of hope in her eyes. 'You'd do that, Cristina? Really?'

'Yes. We'll have to work together: one to keep watch, one to search. And we must be ready, whenever Marius is away from his room.'

'What? More plants? No, Rodric Morgan, enough is enough. I'm amazed we've got away with it this long. And it just doesn't feel right, with kids staying here. We've got to bring this to an end,' said Carys, sitting in her armchair in the only part of Alwyn Hall that felt like her home. The private rooms, where Morgan and Carys lived, were further along the corridor from the kitchen/dining rooms and cloakroom. Morgan sat in a similar chair, his head hanging low.

'I can't see how we get out of it. Not without Marius reporting me to the police.'

'But Marius is committing a crime too. He covered up his boss's murder, and he's a drug dealer,' said Carys, her voice rising with her indignation. 'It's not right, it's not fair,' she added.

'I know that. And now I've got to tell him about this damned book and this lot that are staying here—and God knows what he'll do about all that. Let alone setting up more growing rooms in the tower.'

'Those rooms haven't been used for years. Presumably the one Marius is using is OK? Not that I really care.'

'Yeah,' said Morgan. 'Bit cold and damp, but I've got some heating on. Everything else seemed sound. I'll have to check the other floors.' He sighed. 'I think I'll go and do that now, if he's still talking to his nieces in the kitchen.'

'Just tell him the rooms are unusable,' advised Carys.

'He'll check for himself, so there's no point lying to him,' said Morgan from the doorway. 'I did say he'd have to pay to get the heating installed, and we'd need something to manage the humidity. Maybe that'll put him off. And we can always hope the rooms aren't suitable.'

As Morgan walked along the corridor, he could hear voices in the kitchen. Picking up the keys to the tower doors, he made his way to the tower. Looking up, he could see birds circling the top. *Probably nesting there. More mess to deal with* he thought.

Opening the ground-floor door, Morgan climbed the spiralling staircase slowly. *Have to cut down on the smokes* he thought, feeling breathless by the second floor. He paused before climbing the rest of the stairs, puffing by the time he got to the top. He paused, looking for the key for the top floor room. The lock was stiff from lack of use, and he had to push the door hard to make it open wide enough for him to look inside the room. The tower was something of a folly, built on the whim of the owner in the 19th century.

Morgan looked up at the ceiling. Water stains revealed the leaks from the roof. The floorboards had warped which explained why the door was reluctant to open. There would be some work needed to make this room usable. He checked the facing room, which told the same story of neglect.

On the small landing, a ladder reached up to a hatch door which Morgan knew led out on to the roof. Checking first that the ladder was stable, he started to climb. Fortunately, the hatch lifted fairly easily and Morgan looked out onto the roof: a flat, open area now smothered in a mass of bird droppings and bits of tree. The crenellated stones around the top of the tower were all in place. The wooden floor, where he could see it, looked as though it had seen better days. He wasn't tempted to walk across it to admire the view.

Descending cautiously, he stepped off the ladder and took the stairs to the lower floors, stopping at each level to check each of the rooms. They were not usable as guest rooms, but Marius would probably think they were good enough for his purposes.

Morgan was on the second floor when Marius called 'Hallo? Who's there?'

'Only me,' said Morgan, walking quickly down the remaining stairs. 'Just checking out the rooms on the other floors.'

'And?'

'And they are going to need some work to make them usable. Especially the rooms on the top floor.'

'I check. Give me keys,' said Marius, holding out his hand for them.

'The floor might not be safe in the top rooms, or right at the top of the tower,' warned Morgan.

'Bah, health and safety. Is for babies,' said Marius, grinning.

'If you say so, Marius,' said Morgan, heading back to the main building.

Carys dished out the pie onto three plates, her disapproval apparent in her heavy-handed use of the serving spoon.

'Potatoes? Vegetables?' she asked Marius. Carys finished serving, and sat with Marius and Morgan to eat.

'I look at two floors of tower. Rooms look OK. I check other floors tomorrow,' said Marius. 'You have people staying here?'

'Yes, teachers, I think.' Morgan put down his fork. 'I need to talk to you about them.'

'Why?' asked Marius. Morgan glanced at Carys but she was concentrating on her plate.

'Because … because one of them wrote the book I told you about. And another one drew the pictures for it.' Morgan looked down at his plate, waiting for Marius's reaction.

As Marius took on board what Morgan was telling him, his anger was immediate. ‘What? Why are they here? Why haven’t you dealt with this book?’

‘I thought I had—well, I thought I’d scared off the author so he wouldn’t go ahead with publishing it. But we had a booking, and when they arrived, it was him. And three others. I’ve seen the book, and the drawings the woman made of Alwyn Hall.’

‘Show me,’ said Marius, pushing his plate to one side.

Morgan stood up to get his phone. The scowl on Marius’s face deepened as he looked through the photos.

‘Is easy to see is this place. We do not want it to be famous. You know we have to stop this book.’

‘I know. But I don’t know *how* to stop it.’

‘Bah, you are weak man. I want to meet these people.’ Marius laughed at the worried expression on Morgan’s face. ‘Don’t worry, not to kill. Just talk.’

‘OK. They’re probably out walking somewhere. That’s what they did yesterday. When they come back they will probably go into the dining room to make some tea. You can talk to them then,’ said Morgan.

It was getting colder as the four walkers made their way down the last hill, Gustav in the lead with his tail held high and gently wagging.

‘Are we nearly there?’ asked Jen, grinning to acknowledge she sounded like a small child.

‘Yep, not far now,’ said Aidan, glancing at the map. ‘Hope we can make some tea when we get in. And then, how about going to the pub again this evening?’ There were murmurs of agreement. The four chatted from time to time, and finally reached the road that took them back to Alwyn Hall. Gustav looked a bit downcast at the tarmac, but the others picked up their pace, the thought of tea spurring them on.

In the dining room, the kettle and tea things were set out ready.

Sitting on the bench seats, the four sipped their hot tea gratefully. The door opened, and they looked up, expecting to see Morgan or Carys. But instead, a stockily-built stranger came in.

'Ah hallo. Morgan told me you stay here. I'm Marius,' he said, inviting a hand shake and introductions from the group at the table.

'And this is Gustav,' said Nate.

'Grrr,' said Gustav, his tail low.

'Nice dog,' said Marius, although Nate noticed he avoided patting Gustav. Nate gave Gustav a reassuring pat instead, and the growling subsided to a grumble.

'You like to walk?' he asked. They told him about the walk they had just finished, as Marius made himself a mug of tea. 'I join you?'

'Please do,' said Sam.

'You like this place?' asked Marius. It seemed a good lead in for Aidan to mention his book, and that it would soon be published.

'Ah, you work together?' Marius asked.

'Not exactly, I'm a teacher and I wrote the book, and Jen did the illustrations. Sam works for Phoenix Publishing, the company that are publishing the book. Nate is Sam's friend,' explained Aidan.

Sam frowned as Aidan mentioned Phoenix. She wasn't sure she wanted Marius to know the name. *I'd better warn Charlotte*, she thought.

'And what about you, Marius? What brings you here to Wales?' asked Nate, as casually as he could.

'Morgan and me, we are old friends. He like to ski in my country,' explained Marius.

'Where's home?' asked Sam.

'Romania. You like to ski? Is good. Not expensive. Lots of places.'

'Sounds great. I've never been skiing, but I'll bear it in mind,' said Sam.

'Grrr,' said Gustav.

Cristina could not sleep. How could they get into their uncle's room? Would they find their passports? And if they did, what next? He'd know immediately who had taken them. They'd have to get away as fast as possible. But where could they go?

As she tossed and turned, she became aware of footsteps treading softly on the floor above. Was she dreaming? She lay still and concentrated. There were definitely footsteps. And someone talking, very quietly. Why would Morgan be creeping around in the middle of the night, talking to himself?

She got up, pulling a fleece on over her pyjama top, and put on some socks. Picking up her phone, she quietly opened her bedroom door and peered along the corridor. It was empty. Treading carefully, she started going up the stairs to the top floor. She paused at the top. What if it was Morgan? *I'll just say I was worried someone had broken in* she decided.

She gently turned the handle and opened the door to the top corridor. Two figures were crouched at one of the doors, with a phone flashlight focused on the keyhole. It was two of the people who were staying at Alwyn Hall. She had no idea of their names.

'What are you doing?' Cristina hissed.

There was a clatter as something fell to the floor, and the two figures sprang up in surprise.

'You!' they said in unison.

'What are you doing up here?' asked Nate, frowning at Cristina.

'I heard noises,' said Cristina, 'and came to see who it was.'

'Your English has suddenly improved,' said Sam, looking at Cristina with a puzzled expression.

'Er, yes. What are you doing? Are you trying to get into these rooms?' asked Cristina.

'We know what's in them. Do you?' asked Nate.

'Yes,' said Cristina. 'If Morgan, or Marius find us up here …'

'Sam, go downstairs with her while I carry on trying to get this door open. It was nearly there,' said Nate, bending down to fiddle with the lock again.

'OK, but be quick,' said Sam. 'What's your name?' she asked

Cristina. Cristina told her. 'I think we need to share everything we know. Come to our room, and we can talk.'

'I have to bring my sister,' said Cristina. 'She's called Elena. If she finds my bed empty she will be scared.'

As they passed Aidan's room, the door opened quietly, and Aidan looked out.

'What's going on? Where's Nate? Did you … oh, hello,' he said, spotting Cristina and Elena.

'Get Jen, and we'll meet in mine and Nate's room,' said Sam, whispering. 'But be really quiet.'

Google was not being very helpful. Marius had tried 'Fenix', 'Feenicks', 'Fenit', but nothing came up about a publishing firm. Perhaps the man had given him a false name? Or perhaps he didn't have the correct spelling. English spelling was a mystery. He sighed. Time to phone a friend.

'Morgan, what is this word Feenix?'

'Hello, Marius,' said Morgan. 'Phoenix? It's a bird that rises from the ashes—you know, in myths and legends.'

'Ah, I get it now!' said Marius. 'How do you spell this Fee-nix?' Morgan spelt it out for him. 'Your English spelling. How do you put these letters together and get a word that sounds like Fee-nix?'

'Dunno. But you do. Anything else? If not, I'll see you tomorrow.'

'Ah, tomorrow. Maybe I go off for day. So maybe you don't see me.' Marius ended the call, and keyed in 'Phoenix Publish…' into Google, which immediately offered him 'Phoenix Publishing' and a link to the company's website. Marius browsed the site quickly. There was no announcement about the book he'd seen with the illustration of Alwyn Hall. *Let's keep it that way*, he thought.

Marius slept fitfully, thinking about the day ahead. It would be a long journey to Lower Rushford, but worth it if all went to plan, he decided.

Charlotte checked her phone, hoping for a message from Sam. Nothing. She didn't like to be the first to make contact. After all, she was Sam's boss and she didn't want to intrude into Sam's private time away from work. But she wished Sam would let her know how things were going at Alwyn Hall.

Charlotte made a cup of tea, and picked up her book but she couldn't concentrate. It was still daylight so she got her coat and took the short walk to her office. Everything looked undisturbed and quiet, from the outside, at least. She decided not to go inside. It was getting cold, and she was feeling hungry.

Safely indoors again, Charlotte was stirring the sauce for her pasta supper when she heard the 'ping' of a message arriving. Sam! *All fine here. Keeping safe. Interesting developments. Aidan mentioned Phoenix Publishing to a Romanian man staying here. Dark hair, stocky, called Marius. Not sure if he's involved but be careful. R u OK?*

Charlotte frowned. What did 'interesting developments' mean? *And why might this Romanian be involved?* She replied *Good to know you're OK. Same here. All quiet at office. Look fwd to hearing more.*

There was nothing else she could do … was there? Perhaps she'd go into the office tomorrow just to make sure it was as quiet as it appeared.

Sam quickly introduced Cristina and Elena to the others. 'You speak English, don't you,' Sam said. 'You don't need to pretend with us.'

Looking at Cristina and Elena, Sam realised they were embarrassed. She smiled, trying to reassure them that she wasn't angry with their deception.

'You're not in trouble. We know there's something wrong about this place,' said Aidan.

Cristina looked up. 'We are in big trouble. But it's not our fault, I promise you.'

'OK, tell us how you got here,' said Sam. Jen and Aidan nodded encouragingly.

'OK. I think you know what is upstairs?' said Cristina.

'Yes, we do,' said Sam.

'We are Romanian. We are sisters. The man who is staying here, he is Romanian too. He is our uncle. Uncle Marius,' Cristina paused and glanced at her sister. 'He is not nice uncle.'

'Go on,' said Aidan. 'We met your uncle earlier. He was OK to us.'

'Yes, he is OK when you meet him. When you do what he wants. But he is dangerous. He told us we would have wonderful opportunities in this country. Better than Romania. But we had to work for him first to pay him back the money he spent to get us here. We have worked for him for over two years. We work in kitchen for Carys. And we work for Uncle Marius too.'

'What do you have to do for your uncle? And why is he here now?' asked Sam.

'We deliver packages. A van takes us to the address and we hand over the package. We know what is growing upstairs. The packages have the same thing. And we bring small packages back. We think these are the seeds for Morgan to grow more plants. You see, we are in big trouble,' said Cristina again, her voice wobbling as she finished speaking.

'So why do you do it? Why not go to the police?' asked Aidan.

'Uncle Marius has our passports. We have no papers so the police will arrest us. And Uncle Marius will kill us if we go to the police,' said Elena, taking her sister's hand. 'We want to go home, but how can we?'

The quiet turning of the door handle made them all jump. Closing the door behind him, Nate said 'All done.' He looked at the five people seated around the room and asked 'Everything OK here?'

'This is Cristina and Elena. They're sisters from Romania,' said Sam, going on to explain what the girls had told them.

'Good grief,' said Nate, looking shocked. 'That's terrible.'

'What do you know about Alwyn Hall? And why do you keep coming back?' asked Cristina, looking at Aidan.

Aidan glanced at the others, trying to gauge how much he should tell the girls. 'I think we should share what we know—agreed?' he asked. Nate, Sam, and Jen nodded.

'Well … it's a bit of a long story,' Aidan said, as he went on to explain about the school trip, the idea for his book, the threatening letters, and the knife attack. Cristina and Elena listened, sometimes asking him to repeat something they weren't sure they had understood.

'You must be very careful,' said Elena. 'Uncle Marius will not let anyone stop what he is doing here.'

'Yes, we realise that. But we have to try. And perhaps we can help you to get away from Marius,' said Aidan.

'We need our passports. We think maybe he has them in his room. He sleeps in tower. If we get them we will go home,' said Cristina.

'I'm not sure it's that simple. You've been here a long time, longer than you are allowed now the UK is out of the EU,' said Nate. 'I'd like to think about what we can do. But for now, we should all get some sleep, and perhaps we can talk again tomorrow night.'

'You're right,' said Aidan. 'It's been a long day: it's well gone midnight. Try to sleep. We'll do what we can to help, but keep yourselves safe.'

Nate got up to let Cristina and Elena out, checking the corridor first. It was quiet, and the two girls tiptoed out.

'Gosh, the plot thickens!' said Jen. 'Did you manage to get some photos, Nate?'

'Have a look,' said Nate, opening the first photo on his phone. 'I took quite a few. I don't think there's any doubt that this place is operating as a cannabis farm. And now it looks as though it's being run from Romania.'

'So how's Morgan involved? I mean, why set it up here? And why involve Cristina and Elena?'

'I think we have to talk to Morgan,' said Aidan. Sam, Nate, and Jen looked at him.

'Yes … probably, but let's sleep on it,' said Nate. 'We don't know how he'll react if he feels we've cornered him.'

'Hmm, I think we do … if you'd rather, we could go straight to the police, but I really want to get to the bottom of these anonymous letters,' said Aidan. He yawned.

'I keep meaning to ask you,' said Nate. 'If it was Morgan who sent the letters, how did he know your home address?'

'I wondered that, but when Jen and I stayed here so she could get a feel for the place, I gave my home address on the booking form.'

'That solves one mystery then,' said Nate.

'Only a few more left to sort out!' said Sam.

'Anyway, as you said, Nate, it's late. Come on Jen, let's leave these two to get some rest. Well done though, Nate, those are great photos. And hopefully no one will notice you picked the lock to get them!'

Sunlight broke through the thin fabric of the curtains, waking Sam. Reaching out for her phone, she saw it was still early. Although she'd only slept for a few hours she felt alert. Tyres scrunched the gravel of the driveway, and Gustav's ears twitched. As she got up, moving quietly to the window to see who was leaving so early, Gustav padded softly over to join her. The other vehicle that was parked on the driveway yesterday, was now leaving. It must belong to Marius. Where could he be going at this time of the morning? She scratched the top of Gustav's head, absent-mindedly, and he nuzzled into her hand.

Nate stirred, mumbling 'What are you doing out of bed? It feels like the middle of the night,' he said, not sounding in the best of moods.

'It's just gone six on a lovely, bright morning. I think I saw Marius leaving, although it's a bit early to go sightseeing.'

'All I want to sightsee is the inside of my eyelids,' said Nate. 'Any chance of getting a bit more sleep?' he said, as he rolled over, pulling the duvet up and settling down again

'I'm going out. I'll take Gustav, and we'll bring you up a cup of tea when we get back,' Sam promised, planting a kiss on top of his head. 'Sleep well.' She paused for a moment, looking at him with affection and thinking *And hopefully you'll be in a better mood by then.*

Sam quickly pulled on some clothes, and headed outside into the sunshine, and across the road to take the footpath over the fields. The grass was wet from the dew, and the only sound was of her footfall, Gustav's snuffling, and the singing of skylarks. There was an early morning chill to the air, but it promised to be a warm day. Everything would be idyllic if Sam hadn't got so much on her mind. Thoughts of Aidan's book, Cristina and Elena, cannabis, and Nate vied for attention. She couldn't focus on any of it, so she tried to push it all to one side to appreciate her surroundings. The greenness of the fields, the rising hills backed with blue sky calmed her, while Gustav's methodical investigation of each new smell showed her how to 'be in the moment.' She looked up. If she walked any further she would be climbing the hill which they had gone up yesterday. Sam called to Gustav to go back. He looked at her in surprise, as if to say 'really?' but he soon bounded after her, his tail held high.

Back at Alwyn Hall, Sam made her way to the dining room, hoping to find all she needed to make some tea. As she went in, Carys opened the hatch. They both jumped.

'Come through to the kitchen and have a cup of tea,' invited Carys. 'It's OK, you can bring the dog. I think I've got some treats somewhere.'

Gustav's ears pricked at the word 'treats.' Sam thanked her, and walked round to knock on the door to the kitchen. Sorry,' said Carys, 'it's a bit of a mess in here, but look, here's a chair. I'll just get the kettle on.'

'This is so kind of you—Carys, isn't it?' asked Sam. Carys nodded. 'It must get really busy here when you've got the school groups.'

'It does, but I like having the youngsters around. And that's what we're all about. We're an activity centre so we need the school bookings to make a go of things,' said Carys. 'Here you are. What's your dog's name?'

'It's Gustav. He'll love you forever if you give him a treat or two.'

Carys made a fuss of the dog, and there was a lull in the conversation.

'Have you been doing this for a long time?' asked Sam. 'Running Alwyn Hall, I mean.'

'About five years. I got divorced, and Rodric—or Morgan, as you know him, was made redundant around the same time. Then this place came up so we decided to pool our resources and see if we could make a go of it,' explained Carys as she found mugs and teabags. Picking up a pile of magazines, a few slipped through her fingers, some loose pages flying out and to the floor. Sam got up to help her pick them up.

'That's funny. Someone's been cutting up these pages: there are words missing! Who on earth would do that?' asked Carys, holding up a page with a number of holes in it.

Sam stared at the page. There was no way she could tell Carys of her suspicions. Trying to sound light-hearted, Sam replied 'I've no idea. Maybe someone used them to make an activity of some kind? A teacher, perhaps?'

'Hmm. Maybe,' said Carys, sounding unconvinced. She scooped up the rest of the pages and magazines, and piled them on a shelf of the dresser. 'It's not important. Here you are. There's nothing like the first cup of the day is there,' she said, handing Sam a mug of tea. 'So how are you enjoying your stay here?'

Sam hesitated outside Cristina's door. Before she could knock, the door opened.

'Sam! What are you doing? Is everything OK?' asked Cristina, looking startled.

'Yes, fine. I think I saw Marius drive off in his car earlier, at about six o'clock. I thought you might want to know. He's still not back—or at least, his car isn't parked where it was.'

'Ah, thank you. We will try to get our passports. But if Marius finds they are gone, we will be in trouble.' Cristina looked worried. 'Would you keep them for us? Then if he searches our rooms he will not find them.'

Sam thought for a moment. She wanted to help, but there was a risk that Marius would suspect her or her friends. But it was a small risk, she decided. 'OK, I'll do it. I'll be in my room after breakfast. Come and find me when you've got them.'

'Thank you, thank you!' smiled Cristina. 'You go to breakfast now?' Sam nodded. 'I will wait a few minutes. I don't want Carys or Morgan to know we are talking.'

'OK. I met Carys earlier. She seems really nice,' said Sam.

'Yes, but she is Morgan's sister so we cannot trust her.' Cristina closed her door gently.

Over breakfast, Sam quietly filled Nate, Aidan and Jen in on what had happened earlier that morning.

'So it is Morgan sending the anonymous letters!' cried Aidan.

'Shhh, keep your voice down,' said Nate. 'We need to get hold of those pages. They're evidence. And what are you going to do with the passports, if the girls manage to find them?'

'I'm not sure. Maybe hide them in the campervan?' suggested Sam.

'I don't like the idea of any of us having them,' said Nate. 'If Marius finds out, or if the police get involved, we could be in trouble.'

'I know, but I feel so sorry for those girls.' Sam paused, thinking. 'Maybe I'll hide them in plain sight, and hope for the best. And I won't tell any of you where they are. I'll have a think.'

'Jumping jellybeans, this gets crazier by the day,' cried Jen. 'What next?'

'We need to tackle Morgan,' said Aidan. 'And it might be a good idea to do it while Marius is out of the way.'

'But we've no idea when he'll be back. What if he comes back when we're talking to Morgan? I think we have to try to get Morgan on his own—away from here, ideally.'

Charlotte closed the lid of her laptop with a sigh. Phoenix Publishing was doing rather well, considering it was still early days. She'd had so much to do to bring her company into the 21st century, moving from only printed books to e-books. And then there were changes to make in marketing, using social media, and much more. The team was great, and everyone was learning together. But it did take up a huge amount of her time, at a stage in her life where most people would be thinking about retirement. *Would I have it any other way?* she asked herself. *No. Not until Phoenix is better established.*

Her work had taken her longer than she'd realised but if she was quick, she could pop in to the office to check that everything was as it should be before returning home to prepare some supper. She picked up a jacket and her bag and headed out, enjoying the mid-afternoon sunshine. She was glad she lived within walking distance of her office, even if she did have to resist the temptation to go in outside of normal working hours. Today was an exception: her peace of mind demanded that she checked all was well.

It was easier to take the ironwork staircase that went up the outside of the building to gain access: otherwise, she would have to contend with the revolving door at the main entrance which was heavy and difficult to unlock. She climbed the stairs quickly, unlocking the door to the second floor and went in to turn off the burglar alarm.

It felt strange to be in the office knowing that no one else was there. Even if she popped in at a weekend or evening, there was often someone working extra hours to make sure a book kept to schedule. But today it felt deserted, held on pause until people returned after the bank holiday. *Well, at least there are no dark-haired Romanians* she thought, as she looked into the offices. As she started to go down the stairs she heard a noise. A click. *Must be the heating starting up* she thought.

Charlotte continued down the stairs to the offices on the first floor. Everything appeared to be as she expected: the offices were empty, and workstations in the open plan area were similarly deserted. She smiled to herself as she noted the different ways people left their desks: some strewn with books and papers, while others had nothing more than a keyboard.

Another downward flight of stairs took her to the design studio. Here there were drawings on the wall from various books. Granny Fi, the main character in the long-running children's series, appeared several times. Charlotte paused, remembering her sister who had been the illustrator for the series and who had died because she refused to allow it to go to a publisher in China. She was deep in thought when she realised the door to the corridor was opening. In the door frame stood a dark-haired, bearded man.

'You!' Charlotte gasped. 'Who are you, and what the hell are you doing on my premises? You're trespassing!'

The man waved her words aside. 'You are Charlotte McManners—yes?'

'How do you know my name?' she asked.

'You put your photo on your website. Now, listen to me, Charlotte McManners. You do not need to know my name. Do as I say and you will not get hurt.'

'Hurt? What do you mean?' asked Charlotte, eyes wide in alarm. Her gaze flickered over him, looking for a weapon. There was no gun pointing at her. No knife.

'If you do not follow my instructions people will die.'

'What? What do you want me to do?' asked Charlotte. She tried to keep her voice steady, but her body was tensed, trying to keep her trembling in check.

'Get everything for the book. The *Superswamp* one. Now!' he demanded.

'OK. But why?'

'Do as I say—now!' repeated the man sounding angry.

Charlotte held up her hands, as though to ward off an attack. 'Yes, yes, I'll go and get everything. Do I bring it here?'

'You think I trust you? Ha!' said the man, not sounding amused. 'I follow you. No tricks. No clever moves.'

'OK. Let me think where everything is.' There was a short pause. 'Well, the drawings will be here, in this room. I need to look in the art drawers to see if anything was done as traditional artwork. If not, it will all be on the computer system. And I don't have the access codes for that.'

'Look in the drawers then.'

Charlotte stooped down, and using both hands pulled out the top drawer. It was long, and opened jerkily. She rummaged through the artwork that was mounted on board, each board protected with a layer of translucent paper. There was nothing from *Superswamp* here. She worked her way down each drawer, but each one contained drawings from older series. *Superswamp*'s art must have been created digitally from the outset.

Charlotte looked around the office, quickly checking the cupboards although she didn't expect to find anything. All the time her head was buzzing. *Who was this man? And why the interest in Superswamp? How could she get away from him?* She had the questions, but no answers.

'All the drawings must be on the computer system. I need to go to an office upstairs where I might find some proofs,' she said.

'Proofs? What are these?' Charlotte started to explain but he batted away her words, saying 'Stop talking. Just find everything—quickly.'

Charlotte went back to the first floor, to the Production Manager's office. On the way she checked Sam's desk but there were no proofs. In the Production Manager's office she found a complete set: the whole book, used to make a final check before the book was printed. The proofs were heavy as each huge sheet of paper held several pages of the book and there were multiple sheets of paper. She rolled them up to make it easier to carry them. The man made no move to help her.

'Show me where is computer system,' he demanded.

'You mean, the server?' asked Charlotte. 'It's downstairs.'

'You first. No tricks,' said the man.

Charlotte put the roll of proofs under her arm and headed down to the server room. 'It's here,' she said, indicating a grey door.

'Open it,' said the man.

'I need to get my keys from my bag: it's over there,' said Charlotte, pointing to the desk where she'd stood just a few minutes ago, looking at the *Granny Fi* drawings.

'Get it,' said the man.

Charlotte put the proofs down on the desk to look into her bag.

'I've got the key,' she said, holding it up so he could see it.

'Bring it here. And those pages—what do you say? Proofs?' said the man. Charlotte did as she was told. 'Unlock the door.'

The door opened outwards. Charlotte took a step back and, using the roll of proofs, knocked the man off balance. Charlotte saw her chance and pushed him again, hard. He toppled to the floor as she raced up the stairs. *Damn, the only door that's open is on the top floor*, she thought. She ran as fast as she could, her heart hammering in her ears. Behind her she heard the man curse and get to his feet. Suddenly, her knees buckled as something hit the back of her legs. Her face plunged into the stairs. She just felt the draft of air as something heavy propelled downwards towards her head. She didn't feel the blow that knocked her unconscious.

In the kitchen Cristina and Elena finished putting the clean dishes away.

'Carys, what do we do now?' asked Elena.

'We need to get the rooms ready for schools arriving next week. You know where everything is, so go and make a start.'

'All the rooms?' she queried.

'Yes, all of them. I'll come and help you later. I've got a few things to do down here first. Morgan's gone to the cash 'n' carry.'

Elena sighed. Preparing the rooms would take the rest of the morning, but perhaps there might be a chance to slip across to the tower while Morgan was out of the way and Carys busy indoors. She looked at Cristina who gave a slight nod.

The girls collected together the things they needed for their work and headed upstairs.

'What do you think? Shall we try to get into Uncle Marius's room?' asked Cristina in a whisper.

'I don't know why you're whispering. There's no one here to understand you—only me.' said Elena.

'True! So … shall we?' asked Cristina.

'OK,' agreed Elena. Going back downstairs, she opened the kitchen door. Carys was not there so she quickly took the spare keys for the tower room off the hook.

'Where is Carys?' asked Elena. The sound of flushing water from the downstairs toilet gave her the answer. The girls smiled at each other. 'Let's go!' said Elena.

Marius's room was tidy. He'd made his bed, and left his bag packed. Cristina checked the chest of drawers but it was empty.

'They must be in his bag,' said Cristina.

'There's some pockets on this side—let's check these first,' said Elena. Cristina unzipped the largest pocket and there were their passports. The girls looked at each other in disbelief. It was too easy.

'We have to get out of here,' said Cristina. 'I'm going to find Sam.'

Sam was unlocking the campervan to get Gustav's food. Gustav gave a quiet woof of warning, and she turned to see Cristina and Elena running towards her.

'Sam, we've got them, but we have to get away—now, before Marius gets back,' said Elena, coming to a stop at the campervan. Cristina followed, puffing from the unexpected exercise.

Sam thought for a moment. 'Can you get a few things together? Or do you want me to pack something for you? Wait, go and get a few things and put them on the bed in my room. I'll go up in a minute and find a bag to put them in. No one will query me carrying a bag. Here, give the passports to me.'

'Thank you,' Cristina called over her shoulder as she and Elena hurried away to collect a few belongings. Sam put the passports in one of the campervan cupboards and followed the girls indoors a few minutes later. They had already put a few items of clothing on her bed. Sam found a foldable bag and put everything in it. She stepped into the corridor, checking that it was empty before tapping on their door.

'Go down to the campervan. It's unlocked. Keep out of sight. I'll be down in a minute,' said Sam. The girls nodded, looking scared. 'You'll be OK,' reassured Sam, hoping she was right.

Sam waited a few minutes before going down with the bag. Climbing into the driver's seat, she turned round to say 'Listen, I'm going to take you to a safe place where you can stay for a few days. No one will know you are there. Keep out of sight while I drive out of here.'

The girls, crouching on the floor of the campervan, hunkered down even lower to stay below window height. Sam started the engine, and drove carefully out of the drive, taking the road to Uncle Harry's house.

Nate checked his phone. Nothing from Sam. She'd said she was popping outside after breakfast to get Gustav's food, but that was half an hour ago. Where the hell was she? He'd looked out the window. The campervan had gone, and there was no sign of either Sam or Gustav. He'd sent a couple of messages but he didn't want her to feel he was hounding her—she'd had enough of that from her ex-partner. But he was getting more worried by the minute. *At least she's with Gustav,* he thought.

A sharp knock on the door interrupted his thinking. Sam! He leapt up to open it, only to find Aidan. His face fell.

'Sorry, mate, were you expecting room service?' asked Aidan with a grin, which quickly faded as he took in Nate's troubled expression. 'What's up?' Aidan asked.

'I'm not sure where Sam is. She said she was going to get some food for Gustav. He was with her, but they've both disappeared—along with the campervan. It's been over half an hour. I can't think why she hasn't messaged me.'

'That's not like Sam,' said Aidan.

'I'll have a look around if you like,' added Jen, her frown showing her concern.

Aidan said 'I'll come with you. Do you want to stay here, Nate, in case she comes back to the room?'

Leaving Nate pacing his bedroom like an expectant father, Aidan and Jen stepped outside of the building,

'I'm not sure where to look, with the campervan gone. Maybe we should drive down the road?' suggested Jen.

'Not much point searching the grounds. If Morgan catches us he'll be suspicious. Ah, hang on, I've got a message.' He took his phone out of his pocket. 'It's Nate. Sam's taken Elena and Cristina to Uncle Harry's house. Well, they'll be safe there, but this'll put the cat among the pigeons when Morgan and Marius find the girls have gone AWOL!'

'Might be best to go on our walk as we planned, once Sam gets back,' suggested Jen.

'Yes, it'll give us time to plan how we're going to react when we hear the girls have gone missing. Right, let's have a word with Nate and get our stuff. It might be best if we meet Sam somewhere.'

A few minutes later, Nate, Aidan and Jen loaded the car boot with walking gear for themselves and Sam. Aidan drove carefully, not wanting to miss the layby where Sam had told them she would wait.

'There she is, on the right,' said Jen. 'And I can see Gustav's head.'

'Thank God they're OK,' said Nate, sounding relieved. 'Sam,' he called, 'what's going on?'

Sam gave him a quick hug. 'I'm fine,' she said, 'absolutely fine. I didn't mean to worry you but things happened so fast.' She quickly explained what had happened with the girls. 'They're safe. I left them with some of the food from the camper, and I know there's food in Uncle Harry's freezer as well. So they'll be fine for a few days. Anything happening at Alwyn Hall?'

'No, everything's really quiet, not that it'll stay that way for long,' said Nate. 'You did the right thing to get the girls away. Now we've got to decide what we're going to do about Morgan and Marius.'

'Can we do a walk from here? Who's got the map?' asked Aidan. 'We can talk everything through while we walk. Come on, let's get the boots on and get going. Our brains will work better on the move.'

'You can tell he's a teacher,' said Jen, grinning.

'Right,' said Nate unfolding the map. 'There's a footpath across the road. It takes us up the hill over there. We can make up the rest of the route when we reach the top.'

DC Meera Chaudhury listened carefully, putting down the phone to speak to her boss, DS Balinski. 'Fire at the old Little Bear premises, guv—remember, where they had those death threats last year? The fire crew are just making it safe, but there is a person reported. Looks as though it might be arson.'

'Arson?' queried DS Krystof Balinski, pushing his glasses up his nose. 'They don't have much luck at that place, do they? As I remember it, one of their crazy staff tried to set fire to the MD's garage. Always thought publishing would be a quiet line of work, but not there. Murder, fraud … you name it. And that Inspector got all the credit for solving the case and he didn't even come from here!'

DC Chaudhury smiled to herself. She remembered the case very well. Inspector Keld from the Cumbrian police had got involved as the murder happened in his territory. By solving the murder case, the rest of the pieces fell into place. But DS Balinski had wanted to make his mark and he'd never really forgiven the more experienced Inspector for getting the credit.

'We'd better get over there,' said Balinski, reaching for his jacket. 'God knows what's going on this time. So much for finishing on time this evening!'

As DC Chaudhury parked the car behind the fire engine, she could see in the fading light that the building was still intact, although some windows on the ground floor had cracked, and some debris lay scattered on the ground. Smoke still drifted, the acrid smell of burning irritating her nose. She followed Balinski to talk to the white-helmeted fire officer, who explained the most likely cause of the fire.

'Fortunately, the fire was quite well contained around the server cupboards when we got the call from a passerby who'd smelt the smoke. We had no way of knowing if anyone was inside as there was no one who worked there to tell us. We investigated, and found a body of a woman on the first floor, the floor above the likely source of fire. The pathologist will confirm, but she's taken a blow to the head. Whether that killed her, or whether it was the smoke from the fire, we won't know until the pathologist has made his report.'

'Any idea who she is?'

'No, she had no ID on her. Late fifties perhaps, or early sixties? Probably one of the staff. She might even have started the fire.'

'Possible. What about the cause of the fire?'

'Looks as though something happened with the electrics for the server. We need to investigate fully, of course, to be sure.'

'Wasn't there a fire alarm system?' asked Balinski.

'Yes, but for some reason—which we'll have to look in to—it didn't work.'

'What? That's a bit suspicious, isn't it? queried Meera.

'It is. The alarm goes straight to the fire station, and there's a couple of people who work here who would also be notified.' The fire officer checked his clipboard. 'A Charlotte McManners and a Samantha Holliday.'

'Right. Sam Holliday. I remember that name from the last lot of trouble here,' said Balinski.

'Oh? Well, I'll get on to the pathologist and we'll get identification sorted. Any idea who owns the building?'

'No. I might know more when I've spoken to Charlotte McManners or Sam Holliday,' said Balinski, turning away to get back into the car. As Meera pulled away, he commented 'We'll start with Sam Holliday. See what she knows, and whether she has an alibi.' He looked up at the building. 'I don't think they'll be doing much publishing here for a while.'

They were not short of ideas, which got more imaginative as they started to go up the hill. As the gradient got steeper, the to-ing and fro-ing of suggestions of how they might sort out the Morgan/Marius situation gradually petered out.

'Ouf!' exclaimed Jen, as she took the last step to reach the top. 'Gosh, what a view! I'm completely knackered. My heart wasn't made to beat this fast. And we still haven't decided what we're going to do.'

'We can sit on the stones over there,' suggested Nate. 'Get our breath back and then think everything through.' He waited until everyone had settled themselves, and had drunk some water. Even Gustav settled down, taking a break from checking out all the best smells.

'Now, as I see it,' Nate continued, 'we've got two situations. No, wait, three situations. First of all, Alwyn Hall is operating as both an activity centre and as a cannabis farm. Next, Marius has brought his nieces from Romania and is in effect using them as modern-day slaves, and lastly, Morgan is cutting up magazines to create threatening anonymous letters to stop Aidan's book being published. We've got no evidence that Morgan was the person who attacked Aidan. And we can't prove that Marius is linked with the cannabis, although it looks extremely likely from the messages on Morgan's phone. And now Cristina and Elena are holed up at Uncle Harry's house. Have I missed anything?' asked Nate, looking round the rest of the group.

'Only a decision about where we go next with all this,' said Aidan.

'Well, we could go straight to the police. They'd surely act on the cannabis farm. Nate's photos are proof that someone—Morgan—is growing large quantities of it. There might be bigger fish to catch than Morgan so they might not want to leap straight in. Although a cannabis farm at an activity centre can't be allowed to continue for much longer. I can't believe what Morgan and Carys are doing. They must have got dragged into it somehow,' said Sam.

'We could confront Morgan with the photos and ask him what the hell's going on,' suggested Jen.

'What do we do about Marius?' asked Aidan. 'If he was behind that attack on me, and if he's behind the cannabis business, he will be dangerous. Cristina and Elena seem really scared of him. I don't blame them—he unnerves me!'

'Yes, there's something menacing about him, even when he's trying to be friendly. He just doesn't ring true.' said Nate. 'We need to get hold of those cut-up magazines so we can check that the missing letters correspond with the anonymous messages,' he added.

'How about this?' said Sam. Everyone looked at her expectantly. 'I bet you things will be in chaos once Carys, Morgan and Marius find Cristina and Elena aren't there. No doubt they'll make out the girls are having the day off so we don't suspect anything. One of us could offer to give Carys a hand with the breakfast stuff so that person can get into the kitchen area and smuggle out the magazines.' The others looked a bit dubious. 'Any other ideas?' asked Sam. No one said anything. 'I don't mind volunteering for that.'

'And then we need to get Morgan on his own to show him the magazines and the photos of the cannabis plants, and ask him what the hell is going on here,' Sam continued.

'And Marius?' asked Nate.

'We hope he stays away for a bit. When we've got Morgan's story and more evidence, we'll go to the police,' said Sam.

'Well … it's a plan—of sorts,' said Jen. 'I can't come up with anything better. Unless we just go to the police now?'

'I think we need to go with Sam's plan and get more evidence to be sure the police will take action,' said Aidan. 'Nate, what do you think?'

'Let's give Sam's plan a go,' said Nate. 'It's not watertight, but I don't think we can come up with anything that is. In the meantime, shall we carry on walking for a bit?' He checked the map. 'We can walk along this ridge, then head down and over the fields back to the layby. There's no pub, but we've got some snacks in our packs, haven't we?'

The others nodded. 'It's beautiful up here. Hard to think there's all that stuff going on at Alwyn Hall,' said Jen.

'And there's no more uphill, Jen,' said Sam, grinning at her. 'Just a bit of up and down on the ridge, then downhill.'

'And the difference between 'uphill' and 'a bit of up' is what, exactly?' Jen asked, eyebrows raised.

'Er, well, you just go up a little bit, and then you go down,' said Sam. 'You could say it's 'undulating.'

'Right,' said Jen, 'well, hopefully I can cope with that. It is lovely up here. Look, you can see for miles … oops!'

Gustav went over to her, sniffing at her curiously and looking a little worried.

'I'm all right, Gustav,' said Jen. 'Can one of you give me a hand to get up? It's a bit awkward with my backpack.'

'OK?' asked Aidan, helping Jen to her feet. 'That was quite a big stone to trip over!'

'I know,' said Jen, rubbing her wrist. 'I think I jarred my wrist when I put my arm out to stop the fall. Hmm, it's not too bad but it is swelling up a bit. Perhaps I'll have to go in to the kitchen to ask for some first aid?'

'I like your thinking,' said Aidan.

'What do you mean, 'they've gone'. They can't just disappear! Where would they go *to*?' asked Morgan, looking at his sister in disbelief.

'Ssh, keep your voice down. I don't know if Marius is back yet,' said Carys, a worried frown creasing her brow. 'They were here at breakfast time. I told them to make a start on the rooms for next week's school trips. I went up a while ago to see how they were getting on. They'd only started doing one room, so they must have left quite early. I can't find them anywhere.'

'Where have you searched? The grounds, the tower, upstairs?'

'Upstairs, their rooms, and outside. I'm not going in the tower. I was calling them so if they were in there, they would have heard me. But why would they go in the tower?'

'To see Marius?' Morgan sighed. 'I'll check. Maybe he's back and they're having a cosy chat.'

'Not very likely, is it? They didn't seem to like their uncle very much.'

'Hang on, where's the key? I left it on the hook, right here,' Morgan rattled through the other keys on the hooks but the key to the tower was not to be found. 'Maybe Marius lost his and took this one. I'll go and look.'

Carys sighed. Apart from the mystery of the girls' disappearance, she felt worried about them. And about how she was going to get everything ready for breakfast on her own. What if they weren't back in time to get things ready for next week when Alwyn Hall was nearly full with school groups?

There was a gentle tap on the door. 'Hello?' called Jen. 'Oh, hello Carys. I had a bit of a tumble on our walk, and I was wondering if you had any first aid? Maybe a support bandage for my wrist? Or an icepack to get the swelling down? It's not too bad, but I think it needs a bit of attention.'

'Come on in. We're all at sixes and sevens—it's the girls' day off,' explained Carys. 'Can I have a look at it? Here, sit down and rest your forearm on the table. Hmmm, not too bad. I think you 'll have a bit of bruising. I'll make up an icepack for you, that would be the best thing. Hold on, I'll just pop out to the freezer.'

'Great, sorry to bother you with this,' said Jen. The door to the utility room swung shut, and Jen immediately leapt up and grabbed the magazines on the side of the dresser, and stuffed them into a bag she'd brought for the purpose. She was just fidgeting on her chair when Carys returned.

'Here you are, and an old tea towel to wrap the pack in. You know what to do, don't you? Keep the wrist elevated and use the icepack for no longer than ten minutes. And do keep moving it gently, but not too much. Come and find me if you need another one made up.' Carys held the door open for Jen as she walked out, clutching her bag and the wrapped-up ice pack.

'Oh, Morgan! You made me jump.' Morgan scowled at her.

'This is a private area,' he said.

'I know. Carys was just making up an icepack for my wrist,' said Jen, waving the pack at him. 'See you!' She resisted the temptation to walk too quickly, taking the stairs carefully, and holding on to the banister with the hand of her uninjured arm.

Safely back in her room she took out the magazines and looked at the pages which had words missing. It wasn't possible to immediately tell if the missing words corresponded with the text of the anonymous letters. And Aidan had thrown away the first letter he received. She glanced at her phone to check the time, and spotted 'Phoenix Publishing' in a newsfeed headline. She clicked through and started to read. 'No, oh no, oh poor Sam …' she said aloud. Suddenly she heard voices in the corridor. The others must have heard the news too.

Sam had just finished showering and was wrapping herself in her towel when she heard her phone ringing.

'Would you get that please, Nate?' she called. 'Who is it?'

'No idea. It's showing as a private number. Probably another scam.' It was difficult for Sam to tell who the caller was from Nate's monosyllabic answers. 'Sam,' he called, 'it's DS Balinski, from your local police station. He wants to talk to you,' said Nate, holding the phone out for her to take.

'What?' asked Sam, immediately worried. 'Hello? DS Balinski? Is there a problem?' Nate could hear Balinski's voice, but not what he was saying. But from Sam's shocked, pale face it was clear it was not good news.

'I see. We'd planned to return the day after tomorrow, but we could drive back tomorrow if that helps. Yes …. Yes …. I sent Charlotte a text message yesterday, and she picked that up—I got a reply from her. Yes, that's the right number. Oh God, it couldn't be her … it couldn't be Charlotte who's died, could it?'

Nate looked at Sam in horror, going over to put an arm around her. She looked suddenly fragile, as though she had been physically struck.

'OK, we'll let you know when we expect to get back to Lower Rushford. And you'll let me know if there's any news? About Charlotte, especially.' She ended the call and sat down on the corner of the bed. Gustav pattered over to her, resting his head on her thigh and looking at her with mournful eyes. Sam gave him an absent-minded pat.

'What's going on?' asked Nate. 'What's this about Charlotte?'

Sam looked up, staring into the distance, her eyes unfocused. 'I can't believe it. It can't be true,' she said, more to herself than to Nate.

'Can you tell me? Take your time,' said Nate, sitting next to her and keeping an arm around her. Sam started to shake as the shock set in. She turned to look at him.

'There's been a fire at Phoenix Publishing. The firefighters found a body of a woman in her late fifties or early sixties. The police can't get hold of Charlotte—maybe she's not near her phone or something. Or maybe … maybe it's her,' she said, bringing her hand up to put over her mouth. 'No, it can't be. It's unthinkable,' Sam cried.

'Have you checked your phone? Is there a message from her?' asked Nate. Sam's hands trembled as she swiped her screen to get to her messages.

'Oh no …. No! She texted me while we were walking to say she was going to pop into the office. There's nothing since … around 4. That's not looking good. I'd better let Balinski know.'

'Will it be on the news? If it is, Morgan will find out. And Marius,' said Nate.

'Marius! Oh my God, I'd forgotten … he's not been here all day. Maybe he's behind it all. I wouldn't put it past him! We've got to talk to Morgan and find out what's going on,' said Sam, getting to her feet, looking stronger and more determined.

'Let's tell Aidan and Jen what's happened first. Are you sure you're OK to do this?' he asked.

'Yes. I'll just get dressed, and then we'll talk to them.'

As Sam stepped into the corridor, Aidan's door opened.

'Sam!' he said, looking shaken. 'I've just heard the news …'

'I know. The police called me. They think it's Charlotte—the person they found in the building, I mean,' said Sam.

'Good God, that's terrible,' said Aidan. 'Sam, I'm so sorry.'

'We're just on our way down to speak to Morgan. Oh, Jen, I was about to knock on your door. Looks as though you know what's happened too,' said Sam looking at the horror on Jen's face.

'It popped up on my news feed. Jumping jellybeans, this is crazy. I'm coming with you. We're all going to confront Morgan now, aren't we?' said Jen.

'Try and stop us,' said Aidan, leading the way downstairs.

'Did you find anything?' Carys asked Morgan.

'Nope. No sign of Marius's car. The tower door was unlocked,' Morgan said, holding up the key before putting it back on the hook. 'I found it in Marius's room. Nothing seemed out of the ordinary, but I haven't seen his room since he's been here. And no Elena or Cristina. Have you tried their phones?'

'Of course I have. They've either got no signal, or they've turned their phones off. I suppose they might be out of battery.'

'I don't know what to do,' said Morgan, reaching for his tobacco. 'Everything just seems to get more and more complicated. It's like drowning, slowly.'

Carys looked at his slumped shoulders. She agreed with him, but she didn't think it would help to say so.

'I'll get the meal prepared. You'll feel better after something to eat.' She turned on the radio. 'Although I doubt the news will cheer us up.'

The presenter announced the late afternoon news. Carys started to peel potatoes. Morgan rolled his cigarette.

'A fire at the Cotswolds premises of children's book publishers Phoenix Publishing, has caused extensive damage and left one person dead. The police are not ruling out arson and are currently working to identify the body. The police ask anyone with information about the fire, or about anyone who is missing, to contact them on ....'

There was a clatter as Carys dropped the potato peeler. She turned to Morgan. 'Rodric, that's the place that's publishing that book—the book that's set here. Oh, you're as white as a sheet. What's up?'

Morgan stuttered. 'What's up? What's up?' he repeated. 'Marius was asking me about the publisher. He was Googling them. And today he went off somewhere, and he's not back. And the girls are missing. They have to be involved—they have to be! Oh God, and I was already out of my depth without all this.'

Carys looked at him in disbelief, pulled out a chair and fell into it. 'I just don't believe it. I don't believe it,' she said, wringing the tea towel she was holding between her hands.

'Shut up, woman. I need to think.'

The kitchen was silent, apart from the relentless ticking of the wall clock and the occasional sniff from Carys. The quiet was broken by a knock at the door. Carys and Morgan looked at each other. *What now?* was in both their minds. Morgan got up to open the door.

'You!' he said. 'Look, this is not a good time.'

'We need to talk. Now,' said Aidan. 'Heard the news?'

'Wh-what do you mean?' blustered Morgan.

'Phoenix. Possible arson, and a dead body.' Aidan held up his phone so Morgan could see a photo of the fire-scarred office.

'Never heard of it,' said Morgan.

'Yes you have,' said a voice behind Aidan. 'We need somewhere to talk where we won't be interrupted. We don't want Marius listening in, do we. Where can we go? There's four of us.'

Morgan twitched his pony tail with nervous fingers, and pushed his glasses up his nose. 'Four of you?'

'Yes. So where can we go? Or we can just call the police,' said Aidan.

'No, no, let's not do anything hasty,' said Morgan. 'We can use our flat. It's private. This way.'

Marius drove cautiously, not wanting to draw attention to himself. His clothes reeked of smoke, the smell competing with the stench of his burnt eyebrows. The route on the satnav depressed him. The roads were too busy, and it took forever to get anywhere. Surely London was only a hundred or so kilometres? So why did the satnav say it would take nearly three hours? He sighed heavily and banged his hands on the steering wheel in frustration.

The day had started well enough, despite the long drive from Wales to the Cotswolds. He'd found the building he was looking for easily enough, and by chance he'd seen a woman climb the outside stairs and enter the building on the top floor. He'd parked nearby, and watched her. As she turned to unlock the door at the top of the stairs he recognised her from the photo on the Phoenix website: Charlotte McManners. Good. She would have access to that damned book, and it could all be destroyed, once and for all.

He would enter the building the same way as she had, he decided. He pulled on some thin gloves and started to climb the stairs. He made his way quietly into the building and down to the ground floor. As he expected, there was an alarm system to safeguard against any fires. He quickly disabled it. An out-of-control fire might be the best idea.

He wasn't surprised that Charlotte cooperated. He had that effect on people, and she was no match for his strength. She'd got the huge rolls of paper that she called 'proofs', but the whole computer system had to be destroyed as well. He'd not planned to hurt her—as long as she obeyed his instructions—but she'd tried to trick him. He'd knocked her out, and then she had some kind of seizure. He'd checked for a pulse but there was nothing. *But it was only a light tap. How could she die from that? Any little knock could have killed her. It's just my bad luck it happened now,* Marius thought.

The roll of proofs Charlotte had picked up had started to unravel into a heap of paper that would burn easily. He took out his cigarette lighter and set light to a corner. The flames took hold, moving swiftly to consume the paper. Suddenly, the air filled with acrid smoke. The server was overheating, sparks fizzing and popping. *Bye bye, book*, he thought. *And bye bye Charlotte McManners*. There was no point trying to remove her body. She would be found where she had fallen.

He opened the door to the outside stairs cautiously. The light was fading. He could see no one. He slipped down the stairs and returned to his car. He'd have to lie low for a bit. Once the news got out about the fire, Morgan would know who was responsible. And that would make them quits.

With great reluctance, he picked up his phone and tapped the number to call his boss.

'Constantin?' he said as a gruff voice answered. 'It's me. There's good news and bad news …'

Elena and Cristina went from room to room, not sure what they would find. Sam had briefly told them that the house had belonged to her uncle, and that it was very unlikely anyone would knock the door.

'How can one person have so many things?' asked Elena, looking around the sitting room with its shelves of books, records, and memorabilia. 'Sam's Uncle Harry must have spent years collecting all this.'

'Yes, and I bet there's loads more upstairs,' said Cristina, leading the way up the steep staircase. She opened the first door into a room full of more books, files, papers and photos. 'Hope we find a couple of beds,' she commented.

The next room had a comfortable-looking double bed, stripped of any bedding, and in the third room, a single bed that looked as though it was marooned in an island of books.

'He certainly liked reading,' said Elena, picking up one of the books. *Travels with Charlie*, she read. 'I wonder who Charlie was?'

'Never mind that,' said Cristina, sounding a bit cross. 'We need to find bedding and get these rooms sorted out.'

'You sound just like Carys,' said Elena. Cristina grimaced. 'Do you think we can really be free?' Elena asked her sister, with a wistful tone to her voice.

'I don't know. I hope so. We've just got to wait. It won't be so bad. We've got this whole house to ourselves and no one to tell us what to do. We can speak our own language. We don't have to look at any cannabis plants. Or school children. Or Morgan,' said Cristina.

'Or Uncle Marius,' added Elena, shuddering. 'We just can't go home.'

'Don't even talk about Uncle Marius,' said Cristina. 'Come on, Sam said there's stuff in the freezer to make a meal. It's probably only pizza, but I'm starving!'

'How can you think about pizza? Aren't you even a little bit afraid?' asked Elena.

'What? Of the pizza? No. I might be scared if I we have to eat those terrible fish finger things though.' Cristina looked at her sister's anxious face and made herself smile.

'Idiot,' said Elena, looking a little less worried.

'I'll be right over,' said DS Balinski, ending the call and reaching for his jacket. 'I'm off to the pathology lab,' he called to DC Chaudhury. He adjusted his spectacles and smoothed his hair so it fell slightly more neatly. Meera Chaudhury glanced up from her computer screen. *He's always preening*, she thought. *Not that it does him much good.'*

'Still no reply from Charlotte McManners,' she said. 'There's plenty of photos of her online, if you need them.'

'Send them over to pathology. I don't expect I'll be in until tomorrow,' he said. 'The guv'nor wants an update in the morning, so hopefully I'll have some news.'

'Sam Holliday will be back tomorrow, as well.'

'Yes, she'll need to make a statement. If it is Charlotte McManners who's died, hopefully Sam Holliday can ID the body and help us track down relatives. While confirming her own alibi, of course.'

From the expression on his face, Meera suspected that Krys Balinski would be rather pleased if Sam's alibi *didn't* stack up. It would make a quick, neat end to the case if Sam was the perpetrator, and he was very keen to 'raise his profile'. If she heard that phrase one more time she might scream.

To take her mind off the irritating ways of Krys Balinski, Meera thought back to her encounters with Sam Holliday last year. It was hard to imagine Sam harming anyone, let alone starting a fire that led to a death. If indeed the fire was the cause of death—the Chief Fire Officer seemed to think death occurred before the fire started. *What was Sam's relationship with Charlotte McManners?* mused Meera. *Although that's only relevant if it is Charlotte's body, of course*, she reminded herself.

Her eyes flicked back to her screen. The smiling face of Charlotte McManners looked out at her from a number of images. Meera sighed. Charlotte's life had probably come to an untimely end. She hadn't even had a chance to retire. *You're getting maudlin,* she thought to herself. *The best thing to do is to find the person who took her life.* She steeled herself to select a couple of images that showed Charlotte's face best, and sent them over to pathology. She shut down her computer. Tomorrow promised to be a long day.

Morgan led the way along the corridor to the ground-floor flat he shared with Carys. A feeling of utter exhaustion swept over him. He'd tried so hard to do Marius's bidding, and to keep Alwyn Hall running as an activity centre. And now, despite all his efforts, it was about to fall apart. *How much do they know?* he wondered.

He unlocked the door to the flat, and as the others followed him in, he went to sort out chairs for everyone. The others stood, waiting, uncomfortable being in Morgan and Carys's home. The furnishings were old-fashioned, with floral patterned covers on the two armchairs. An old dresser leaned against the wall, and a small television occupied one corner. The carpet in front of the armchairs looked worn. *If they're making money out of the cannabis they're not spending it on home comforts* thought Sam.

Taking the chairs from Morgan, the four friends positioned themselves in the space between Carys and Morgan's armchairs. Morgan looked at them, his expression wary. Carys looked frightened.

'Look, we've got a pretty good idea what's going on here, but we want to hear it from you first,' started Aidan.

'Don't know what you mean,' said Morgan, his fingers tapping his leg. He'd left his tobacco in the kitchen.

Aidan sighed. 'OK, let me spell it out for you. I've written a book. I got the idea for it when I stayed here with my school. Jen drew the illustrations, and the place where the story is set is recognisable as Alwyn Hall. We've acknowledged Alwyn Hall on the back cover. You know all this.'

Morgan yawned and started to get up from his chair. 'So why are you telling me? I've got work to do. I can't sit around here nattering, however fascinating your book is to you.'

Aidan quickly got up and pushed Morgan back into the armchair. 'Sit down. You're not going anywhere. You didn't like Alwyn Hall being in the book. In fact, it was much more than not liking it. 'Kill the book or we kill you' was your way of putting it—wasn't it?'

Morgan shrank back in his seat. 'What? You've got no evidence. You can't go around accusing me!'

Carys clamped her hand over her mouth as she realised the significance of the cut-up pages of magazines in the kitchen. 'Oh no, Rodric,' she said.

'Shut up, Carys,' said Morgan. 'He can't prove anything.'

'He can, actually,' said Jen. 'We've got the magazines you used to cut out the letters.'

Morgan threw her a look that would make paint bubble but Jen held his gaze. 'I think you should tell us what's going on,' she said.

'That's good advice,' said Nate. 'Because we know about the cannabis too.' There was a quiet moan from Carys, who sat in the chair with her hands over her face, rocking backwards and forwards.

Morgan was white. 'You *know*?' he said.

Nate showed him one of the photos of the cannabis-growing rooms that he had on his phone. 'Strong, healthy plants. You've made a good job of it, Morgan. Must make you a fair bit of money. Not sure what you spend it on though,' he said as his eyes flickered around the shabby room.

Morgan snorted. 'Money? It's not me who makes the money.'

'So who does? Who's getting rich on running a cannabis farm at an activity centre for schoolchildren?' asked Sam.

Morgan winced. 'Don't say it like that. Do you think I wanted to do it? Carys and me, we made a good living from the activity centre. Not a fortune, but enough to be comfortable. We even had a couple of holidays.' He paused. He looked defeated, with no energy left for blustering.

Aidan saw his opportunity. 'Go on,' he said. 'You didn't want to grow cannabis. What about the anonymous letters? The threats? The attack in the school playground—that was you, wasn't it? I suppose you're going to say you didn't want to do any of that either but you *did* do it.' He leaned forward, his anger giving him a menacing look.

Morgan could not meet Aidan's eyes. Shoulders slumped, his gaze turned downwards, Morgan was a picture of abject misery.

'Oh, Rodric,' said Carys softly. 'You're going to have to tell them,' she said.

Morgan looked up at her. He knew she was right. He sniffed, pushed his glasses up his nose and said 'OK, OK, I'll tell you how it all came about. It's a long story.'

'We're listening,' said Sam. The four friends all looked at Morgan, waiting to hear the secrets of Alwyn Hall.

May 2024

Morgan sat back in his armchair. 'It started with a skiing holiday in Romania …'

January 2022

It could be as much as 80% alcohol, or so he'd heard. Morgan sniffed the tendrils of steam that were drifting up from the glass he was hugging between his chilled hands. He raised it to his lips, sipping tentatively. The homemade brandy caught the back of his throat and he tried to stifle the cough. His companion looked on in tolerant amusement.

'What's in this?' asked Morgan. 'It's potent stuff.'

'You like?' Marius asked, as Morgan started to take another sip.

'I think so.' Morgan sipped carefully, licked his lips and the edge of his moustache, and smiled. 'Yeah, I do. Plums?'

'Is our national drink,' said Marius, standing taller as he spoke. 'Is not so strong to us. Is like medicine for you.'

Morgan spluttered. 'I'd better not have too much. I've got to drive to Bucharest later.'

Marius laughed, white teeth gleaming in his dark beard. He towered over Morgan, a bear of a man. He took a sip of his own drink. 'This one just 40%, not so strong. You go home today?'

'Yeah, got a late flight back. I was just having a last run before packing. No more skiing for me once I get home.'

'You ski good,' said Marius.

'I was doing all right until I spun off at that bend,' said Morgan, rubbing his arm where he'd jarred it, trying to keep his balance. 'Thanks for helping me.'

'No problem. I was in right place at right time.'

They stood at the cabin that sold the drinks, chatting. The usual holiday small talk. Drink finished, Morgan shook hands with Marius and returned to his hotel to pack. Morgan's arm throbbed, but the shock of the near fall was wearing off, helped by the plum brandy. A quick nap later, he finished packing up his clothes and skis, and phoned reception to organise getting his hire car out of the underground garage.

It was getting dark now, and snow was steadily falling. The mountains where he'd spent the last week skiing were silhouettes, their jagged beauty shrouded in the half-light of dusk and the snow. It had been his sister's idea to come to Romania. She knew how much he enjoyed skiing, but it was usually expensive even though snow was not guaranteed. Romania was a revelation: cheap flights, an inexpensive ski resort, and a good mix of runs that catered for all levels. He was sorry to leave, but it was time to load up the car, and head downhill to the airport.

He drove steadily, mindful of the brandy. The temperature was dropping and the road was icy in patches. He hadn't seen much traffic, but there was now a vehicle coming towards him. As the oncoming car approached him, it suddenly swerved, going off the side of the road. Morgan pumped his brakes and brought his car to a halt. Heart thudding, he realised that if the car had swerved the other way, it would have hit him.

The seat belt had done its job, yanking Marius back into his seat, jolting his whole body. No bones broken. No bleeding. He looked into the front seats, partly lit by the headlights of the other vehicle. The driver was slumped over the steering wheel, unmoving. The old car had no airbag. The front passenger footwell was full of bags which was why Marius had opted for the back seat. It had been a lucky choice.

Marius tried opening his door. Putting his shoulder to it, he gave it a shove and almost fell into the snow as the door suddenly opened. He stepped out onto the icy road and forced the driver's door open. The driver sat motionless. He felt for a pulse, his nose wrinkling at the iron-like smell of blood. No pulse.

He walked carefully to the other vehicle, pulling open the driver's door, using the torch on his phone to shine it on the driver's face. The driver opened his eyes, immediately putting up his hand to shield them from the bright light.

'You! We meet again,' said a voice Morgan vaguely recognised.

'Marius?' Morgan asked, tentatively. 'What the hell's happened?'

'You killed my boss,' said Marius. 'Get out.'

Morgan shrank from him. 'What? But he was the one who swerved for no good reason! It wasn't my fault—he must have hit some ice! I haven't killed anyone. You've got to believe me, Marius.'

'He swerve to miss you. I am—how do you say? The person who sees what happens. Now he's dead. I call my brother now. He has farm near here. He bring truck.' Marius tapped his phone and spoke rapidly to the person who answered it.

'My brother, he come with truck. We wait here.'

'We'd better check on your boss,' said Morgan, easing himself out of his seat. Everything ached, but at least he could move. 'He might be alive.'

'He's dead, I tell you,' said Marius, going round to the driver's side of the vehicle he had travelled in.

Morgan trod cautiously over the slippery road and looked through the window at the other driver who was slumped over the steering wheel. He saw a man who was probably in his forties, bearded, with receding dark hair, and a small scar that made a dip in the shape of a small dish on his temple. Marius turned on the flashlight on his phone. There was no reaction from the driver. Morgan touched the driver's shoulder, and the man slumped more towards the gear lever.

'You checked for a pulse, did you?' asked Morgan.

'Yes. Nothing. I tell you, he's dead.'

'I'm so sorry, Marius,' said Morgan. He stepped back and pushed the car door closed. It was bitterly cold, and Morgan started to shake.

'Sit in your car,' said Marius.

Within a few minutes, Morgan heard the sound of a truck engine. After a brief exchange, the truck driver started to load the damaged vehicle, with the body inside, on to the back of his low-bed truck.

'What's he doing? We should call the emergency services for the driver. We might be wrong,' said Morgan in disbelief.

'You want police? You want prison?' said Marius. Morgan looked at him, the full horror of his situation dawning on him as he took in the scowl on Marius's face. 'No. I think you don't. We drive to farm—now,' and he got into the front passenger seat. 'You follow truck.'

Morgan looked at the man now sitting next to him. The man who had been so kind after Morgan had fallen on the ski run. He didn't seem friendly now.

Morgan pulled up in front of the farmhouse and turned off the car engine.

'Give me keys,' said Marius.

'What?' asked Morgan. 'Why?'

'You killed my boss. You do not ask questions,' said Marius, taking the keys from Morgan. 'Get out of car and follow me.'

Morgan followed Marius to the farmhouse door. Marius banged loudly on it, although the farm dogs had heard their approach. As the door opened, two large hounds leapt out, barking at the Morgan and Marius. Marius called them by name, and the dogs quietened, snuffling at the men's heels as they followed them into the house.

Despite the warmth of the kitchen-cum-sitting room, Morgan shook with cold and shock. Marius spoke a few words to the people sitting around the table. An older man had opened the door; his wife and two daughters remained seated at the table. Morgan felt their curiosity, and tried to smile but his knees buckled and he staggered as he tried to keep his balance. Marius grabbed him, and steered Morgan to an empty chair at the table, barking out some instructions in Romanian. The older woman got up, taking a small glass from the cupboard and filling it with a rich-red liquid. Plum brandy.

'Drink. Is good for shock. These people are my brother and his family. I tell them what happened. You stay here tonight.'

'But I've got to get to the airport. I've got a flight back to London,' said Morgan, picking up the glass in a trembling hand.

'You have no flight. You go nowhere. You must not drive. You stay here. We talk later.'

Morgan looked at Marius's stern face. He had no choice.

The woman slid a plate of meat and potatoes in front of him. Morgan wasn't sure he could eat, but she indicated that he must at least try. He attempted some of the meat. She passed him some bread. The meat was tasty and tender, and he'd soon finished it all, even wiping round the plate with the bread. The woman smiled, eyebrows raised as though asking if he wanted more. Morgan shook his head.

'Good. Now we talk,' said Marius. Morgan felt slightly sick. He couldn't think clearly, his head fuzzy with shock and plum brandy.

'I take your car to hire company. The paperwork is in car, yes?' Morgan nodded. 'OK, you stay here for few days. You have family, wife?'

'No wife,' said Morgan. 'Just my sister. I live with my sister.'

'Here's your phone. You message sister. Tell her you decide drive home. You not be home tomorrow. You understand?'

'Not really,' said Morgan. 'I didn't kill your boss. You can't keep me here. I've got to get to the airport.'

Suddenly, Marius turned, his face dark red and almost touching Morgan's. Morgan could see a vein twitching just above

Marius's eye. 'You do as I say, or I call police. You go to prison—yes?'

Morgan pulled away. 'No—no, not prison.'

Marius leaned back, jabbing his forefinger into Morgan's chest as he said 'You listen. Listen carefully. This is what you do.'

Morgan pulled the heavy blankets around him, trying to get warm in the cold bed. He had seen his breath as he took off his trainers and dithered about removing any of his clothes. In the end he'd simply pulled back the blankets and climbed into bed fully dressed.

In his head he heard Marius's voice, explaining what he had to do if he wanted to leave Romania a free man. Marius said he'd take care of the hire car. He'd take care of the body. How could he do that? Wouldn't people wonder where this boss had got to? Who exactly was Marius?

In return, Marius said, Morgan would work for him. 'Working from home' Marius had said with a smirk. Morgan didn't like the sound of this work. He didn't trust Marius, and clearly Marius distrusted Morgan. Otherwise, why had he said that the two young women he had met earlier would be living with Morgan and his sister. Marius was like a spider, spinning a web around him that made Morgan feel more and more trapped.

Exhausted, Morgan eventually slept, jolting awake at a knock on this door. The older woman had a mug of coffee for him. He got up and took it from her. The simple kindness was almost more than he could bear.

Carys knocked tentatively at the bedroom door. 'Rod,' she called, quietly. 'Rodric! Want a cup of tea?'

'Go away.'

Carys sighed. She'd hoped that after a week's skiing her brother would be in a more relaxed mood. But since he came home a couple of days ago he'd been quiet to the point of surliness. Even with his usual glass-half-empty temperament, he wasn't usually grumpy for this long.

She called him Rod, saving his full name, Rodric, for when he annoyed her. Everyone else knew him by their family name, Morgan. She couldn't remember why. He'd been Morgan since his schooldays.

He'd messaged her on the last day of his holiday to say he'd decided to take a longer break so he could drive back. Why? Who would want to drive from Romania? He'd had a return flight ticket. And he hadn't seemed to enjoy the drive. Not that he'd talked much about it, even when she'd asked him. Fancied the challenge, he said. He'd messaged her again to say he was stopping in the outskirts of London. That can't have been easy, driving around those streets. *What on earth had possessed him?* she asked herself for the umpteenth time.

She'd tried asking about the skiing but she couldn't get much out of him about that either. Downstairs in the kitchen, she poured herself a cup of tea and waited for him to get up.

Morgan got up slowly, his body still stiff from the last few days. His head throbbed but he had to move. There was so much to do. He'd managed to unload the car and get the stuff upstairs without Carys seeing. But it would be impossible to keep it a secret for much longer.

In the kitchen, Carys sat at the table, her foot tapping the floor, thinking how she could get Morgan to talk. She started as he lay his hand on her shoulder.

'Sorry,' said Morgan, squeezing her shoulder with unexpected gentleness.

'So you should be,' she said, giving him a sharp look. His face was pale, rings dark under his eyes. In a softer tone she added 'I'm worried about you.'

'Yeah, I know,' said Morgan, tying his hair back into his usual ponytail.

'Tell me what's going on. And don't say 'nothing' because I know you too well.'

Morgan reached for the teapot, pouring himself a mug of tea. 'It's a long story,' he said.

'I'm listening,' said Carys.

Morgan went over to the kitchen drawer and took out his pouch of tobacco and cigarette papers. He heard her tut of disapproval. 'I know, but when you hear what I've got to tell you, you'll understand.'

'Two girls! We've got to find room for two girls?' asked Carys, her voice rising in pitch. 'And we have to turn the top floor into some kind of greenhouse? What's all this going to mean for our business—because we've still got this place to run as an activity centre.'

'Yeah, I know, it's a lot. But that's the deal. Someone died in a car accident I couldn't prove wasn't my fault. And I'd had the brandy. Apparently drinking any alcohol and driving is a criminal offence in Romania. Marius was right, it would have meant a prison sentence, and staying in a Romanian jail didn't hold much appeal,' said Morgan.

'No … no, I get that,' said Carys. 'But he's blackmailing you. And what we're doing is illegal. It's all wrong, having children staying here while we're growing cannabis. We'll go to prison if we're caught.'

'Yeah, I know all that, Carys. But this Marius, he's a nasty piece of work and he's got me over a barrel. According to him, I'm responsible for killing his boss and Marius's silence comes at a price,' said Morgan, stubbing out his roll-up in a saucer.

'No wonder you've started smoking again,' commented Carys with a sniff. 'So we have to grow this—this stuff, and the girls will deliver it to wherever Marius tells them. And if that's all OK and the girls give Marius a good report you'll be safe? And these girls are his nieces?'

'Yeah, nieces, apparently. And yes, that's the deal,' said Morgan.

'Why are the nieces going along with this?'

'Because he's sold them the idea of working in the UK. The

alternative is that they stay on the farm with their father, Marius's brother. I got the impression that they think coming to the UK is an adventure, the start of a new life,' explained Morgan, trying to keep his patience.

'My God, so much for a cheap holiday. I wish I'd never mentioned Romania. How long do we keep doing all this for?

Morgan shrugged and said 'Until Marius says we can stop.'

'And why would he do that? I mean, we're making everything easy for him, aren't we? So why would he say 'oh it's OK now, you've paid off your debt to me? I just don't see how we'll ever get out of it.'

'I dunno. We'll have to work that out later. Right now, I'd better check on the plants. And the heating. I've got a lot to organise. Oh yeah, the girls get here later this week.'

May 2024

There was silence as Morgan finished speaking.

'I don't know what to say,' said Aidan. 'That's quite a story.'

'It's true,' said Carys. 'We never wanted to do any of this, but neither did we want Morgan to end up in prison in Romania.'

'I think you're going to have to bite the bullet and tell the police everything. If it is Charlotte McManners' body, and if Marius killed her, then I don't see what else you can do—whatever it's going to mean for you.'

'Maybe we can just lie low?' asked Morgan. 'Although I can't see how I'll ever escape from Marius.'

'He can't keep you in his clutches, especially if he's killed someone too,' said Jen.

'He'll come back here though,' said Morgan. 'He'll try to bluff his way out of it.'

'That's why we've all got to make a stand against him. Maybe this isn't his only cannabis farm. He could be doing more harm than we can imagine with his drug trade,' said Jen. 'By the way, has he been in touch with you since he left this morning?'

'God, was it only this morning? Er, no, he hasn't,' said Morgan. 'What about Cristina and Elena? They've disappeared. Is that

Marius's doing as well? Were they involved with what happened at Phoenix Publishing?'

'Maybe with Marius out of the way, they've just run away?' suggested Sam, avoiding eye contact with any of her friends. 'Were they close, do you know—Marius and his nieces, I mean?'

'Close!' snorted Carys. 'Definitely not. You could feel their dislike of him when they were together: dislike mixed with fear.'

'Yes, Marius was very intimidating, even when he was pretending to be nice,' said Sam.

'Look,' said Nate. 'Why don't we sleep on it, and contact the police in the morning. Nothing's going to change overnight, although Marius might come back here which would make it easier for the police to arrest him.'

'True,' said Aidan. 'I'm OK with that. Morgan? Carys? There's no point trying to make a run for it, is there!'

Morgan looked at him with a small smile. 'I know,' said Morgan, sounding resigned. 'But I want to keep Carys out of this as much as possible. None of this was her doing. And look, I'm sorry about the letters, and going for you in the school playground. Marius got me between a rock and a hard place.'

Aidan looked at Morgan in surprise. 'Yeah, I can see that.' *Maybe there's a few grains of decency in him after all,* Aidan thought. *But then he threatened me with that knife … would he have used it if I'd tried to get away? He's weak, which makes him unpredictable when he feels threatened,* decided Aidan. *I'm not going to feel too sorry for him.*

Nate looked at Sam. She looked drawn and tired. Tomorrow was going to be a long day, with the journey back to Lower Rushford for her appointment with DS Balinski. *This is all too much. And goodness knows where we'll find the local police station to speak to someone about the cannabis* wondered Nate.

'OK, we'll leave you in peace for now,' said Aidan. 'I'll talk to you again first thing tomorrow. We'll see ourselves out.'

Morgan looked up at him and nodded. Carys dabbed her nose with a tissue she'd found up her sleeve. The four friends trooped out, one behind the other, in silence.

'Well …' started Jen.

'Shhh,' said Aidan, shaking his head at her. 'Wait until we're upstairs,' he hissed. At the top of the stairs he indicated that they should go into his room. The four perched on the edge of the beds.

'Jumping jellybeans, that was one crazy story Morgan told us,' said Jen as the door closed behind her. 'Did you believe him?'

'I did, actually,' said Aidan. 'It was just like Morgan to be the wrong bloke in the wrong place.'

'That Marius is a nasty piece of work: a blackmailer, drug dealer, and now probably a murderer, if he wasn't already,' said Sam, shuddering. 'Poor Cristina and Elena.'

'How are they? Have you heard?' asked Nate.

'No. I thought it best if they kept their phones off, just in case Marius tries to contact them—which he will, eventually,' said Sam.

'Are you OK, Sam?' asked Jen. 'Sorry, stupid question. You must be really worried about Charlotte, let alone those two girls.'

'I wish I knew if it was Charlotte they found … and then I think I don't want to know. It's terrible. I liked her—I liked her a lot. And goodness knows what it'll mean for Phoenix Publishing if she has died.'

'Let's take this one step at a time,' said Nate. 'Tomorrow, you've got to be back in Lower Rushford, Sam. How about you and Jen go together, and Aidan and I will stay here to keep an eye on Morgan, especially if Marius shows up. Aidan and I'll go to the local police and get the ball rolling about the cannabis. It's not looking good for Morgan, but we can't turn a blind eye to what's going on here.'

Sam opened her mouth to protest about making the journey without Nate, but she could see there was good sense in his proposal so she didn't argue. She would welcome Jen's company on the journey home.

'No heroics, you two,' Sam said in a firm voice. 'It would be best to go to the police early, before Marius gets here—assuming he doesn't arrive overnight.'

'Agreed. We'll all make an early start,' said Nate.

'Come on, I'm feeling peckish now. I don't think we want to go out for a meal, so why don't we pool our snacks and have a bit of a picnic in here?' suggested Aidan.

'Good call,' said Jen. 'I'll go and get my biscuit supply, and some chocolate bars.'

'Aha! I thought I could count on you for a secret stash of goodies,' said Sam, sounding more light-hearted than she felt. 'I've got some malt loaf and cheesy biscuits, and there might be a few brownies left,' she added.

'Leave some for me. I'm just going to get Gustav and take him out for a quick walk,' said Nate.

'Oh no! I'd completely forgotten about poor old Gustav. Bring him in here when you come back. He'll be glad of some company,' said Aidan.

The call to Constantin was short and bad-tempered. While Constantin was pleased to hear that it was very unlikely the book could now be published, predictably, he was not at all pleased that it had taken a murder to bring this about.

'You'll have to lie low,' said Constantin. 'You know the collection point for the seeds. Go there, and keep your head down until we find out how much the police know. We need to keep the business going, even if I have to get a flight to London to sort it out.'

That was the last thing Marius wanted. He knew his life counted on his ability to convince Constantin he was strong and could run the UK business well. He set up the satnav to return once again to outer London.

Sam packed her things quickly, feeling glad she had not brought too much with her.

'Maybe when this is over we can have a bit of time to ourselves,' said Sam.

'That would be good,' said Nate with feeling. 'I thought I'd left crime scenes behind when I came out of the police force. If we can grab a few days with no murders or mysteries to solve, that would be wonderful. Even in the campervan!' he grinned, and pulled Sam into a hug to kiss her goodbye. He felt Gustav's nose bump against his leg. 'Yes, Gustav, we haven't forgotten you. A quiet few days with some walks, we promise,' he said. 'I'm sure Gustav understands everything we say, you know.'

'Oh, Gustav,' said Sam, bending down to make a fuss of him. 'It hasn't been much fun for you, has it. We'll give you our undivided attention very soon. And you're to look after Nate for me.'

'Woof,' agreed Gustav.

'I'll give you a hand with your stuff. If you want to give Jen's door a knock, I'll see you both down at the camper.'

A few minutes later, Sam and Jen were on their way. 'I need to let Cristina and Elena know what's happening,' said Sam, as she drove quickly on the quiet road. 'We won't stop long.'

The two bleary-eyed girls looked at Sam and Jen in disbelief as they listened to Sam's update on yesterday's events.

'Just stay here, as you've been doing,' said Sam. 'Nate and Aidan know you're here. So don't worry, someone will keep you updated and we'll sort out what your options are.'

'Thank you, Sam,' said Elena, giving Sam a hug. 'You are good friend to us,' Sam smiled, hugged Cristina, and returned to the campervan.

The journey to Lower Rushford felt long, despite the quiet roads. It was still only eleven when Sam pulled up outside her house.

'Here we are. Do you want to make some coffee while I call DS Balinski? I desperately need some caffeine after that drive.'

Jen slid a mug of coffee in front of Sam who was listening intently to DS Balinksi. 'I see,' said Sam, sounding very subdued. 'Yes, 12.30, if that's OK?' She ended the call and said 'It looks very likely that the body is Charlotte's. Balinski's asked me … .' She coughed to mask the wobble in her voice. 'To identify the body.'

Jen put out a hand to squeeze Sam's arm. 'I'll come with you,' she said.

'Thanks. I've also got to make a statement. You'll probably need to do one too. We're going to be there for quite some time. Oh, wait, there's a message from Nate.' She scrolled down and gave a small gasp.

'They're heading over to the police station: Nate, Aidan, Morgan and Carys. No sign of Marius.'

'I wonder where he's hiding? Once the police hear about what's been going on, he won't be able to leave the UK without being caught,' mused Jen.

'I don't know. Right, let's finish our coffee and get over to the police station. I need to get this over and done with.'

Inspector Huw Bevan waited while the whirring of the machine eventually produced a cup of muddy liquid that claimed to be coffee. He sighed. Despite telling himself he was never going to drink another drop, he still found himself standing at the machine every morning, resenting the coffee and his need of it.

Returning to his desk, he settled down to completing a report that was supposed to be ready for a meeting tomorrow. He looked up as the duty officer called over to say there were four people at the front desk who wanted to talk to him. They insisted on seeing the senior officer.

'What's it about—any idea?' he asked.

'They wouldn't say. I think I recognise one of them, but I don't think the others are from around here.'

Bevan sighed and went out to the front desk to meet them.

'Good morning. I'm Inspector Bevan. I understand you want to talk to me?' His eyes took in the four people as he spoke: a small woman in her fifties who looked terrified, a miserable-looking fifty-something man with a greasy pony tail and nicotine-stained moustache, and two younger men who had a quiet air of authority and looked completely out of place in a police station.

'Hello, yes, good morning. I'm Aidan Wilcox, and this is Nate Braithwaite, Rodric Morgan, and his sister Carys. Is there somewhere we could go to talk to you? It's a bit sensitive.'

'This way,' said Bevan, leading the way down a brightly lit corridor, devoid of anything on the wall to alleviate the starkness. The building looked new, and there was still a faint smell of paint.

'Right, come in here and sit down. What's this about?'

The four sat around the small table in the middle of a meeting room, with Bevan at the head. Morgan and Carys shuffled in their seats and kept their eyes down. Aidan and Nate looked at each other. 'Shall I start?' asked Aidan. Nate nodded.

'OK, well, bear with me, Inspector Bevan. Thank you for agreeing to meet with us. What we have to tell you involves cannabis, blackmail, murder, or at the very least, manslaughter, as well as two young women who have been prevented returning to their home country,' started Aidan.

'That's quite an opening,' said Bevan. 'You've definitely got my full attention. Carry on in your own time.'

Aidan gave him a small smile. 'Thanks.' He paused, thinking how best to explain all that had happened. 'I suppose it's best to start with the school visit to Alwyn Hall. Do you know where that is?' asked Aidan, sounding a little uncertain. The Inspector nodded. 'I'm a teacher, and I went with my Year 6 class and some colleagues to Alwyn Hall in January 2023. Nothing out of the ordinary happened, but we all commented that there was something a bit weird about the place ...'

Sam stood away from the body, her hand to her mouth.

'Yes. Yes, it's her ... It's Charlotte McManners,' she stuttered.

'Thank you. Come on, let's get you out of here and find you a cup of tea,' said the mortuary assistant.

Sam nodded, not trusting herself to say anything more. Out in the corridor, she found Jen waiting for her. From her face, Jen knew immediately that Sam had just identified Charlotte's body.

'Oh, Sam, I'm so sorry,' she said, giving her friend a hug. 'How awful.'

'It's awful that she's dead, but to think someone did this deliberately is just … well, it's just unbearable,' sobbed Sam into Jen's shoulder.

'Come on, let's get some tea before we see Balinski,' said Jen.

'There's a machine a bit further down this corridor. I'll come with you, and show you the room where you can wait,' said the assistant.

Jen and Sam sipped their teas, waiting, thinking their own thoughts. There was a quiet tap on the door and Balinski came in.

'Good morning, thank you for coming in. I understand you've just formally identified Charlotte McManners. Thank you for doing that—I know how difficult it must have been, and I'm sorry for your loss.'

'It's probably the worst thing I've ever had to do,' said Sam, the slight tremor in her voice betraying her emotion. 'She was a lovely woman. I can't believe she's gone, and in this way.'

'We'll get whoever did this to her,' said Balinski, sounding confident. 'And that's where I'm going to need some further help from you. And who are you? I think I know you, don't I?' he asked, looking at Jen.

'Oh, sorry, I'm Jen Somerville. I used to work at Phoenix. I'm the one who draws the caricatures. But I'm freelance now. Sorry, I'm waffling. I was with Sam in Wales when she got your call.'

'I think we'll need to talk to you as well then,' said Balinski. 'OK, Sam, do you feel ready to make a start?' Sam nodded. 'Good. Let's go through to the interview room. Jen, stay here please and I'll ask my DC to talk to you. This way, Sam.'

After an hour, Balinski suggested they stopped for a short break. Sam felt exhausted. She had explained everything that had happened three times now. Each time, Balinski stopped at different points to ask questions. She was starting to question herself.

The tea revived her. Balinski returned, taking the chair opposite her.

'It's quite a story,' he said. 'Why didn't you report it to the police sooner?'

'Aidan—the author—did report the anonymous letters, and the attack in the school playground. As I said, he and Nate Braithwaite have stayed on at Alwyn Hall so they could go to the local police station with the people who run Alwyn Hall.'

'And you think this Marius character has tried to stop the book being published by murdering the owner of Phoenix Publishing, and starting a fire on the premises?' asked Balinski. Sam nodded. 'And who gains from Charlotte McManners' death?'

Sam's shocked eyes locked with Balinski's. 'What? What kind of question is that?'

'A routine one, in this type of situation,' said Balinski, showing no hint of sympathy. 'Please answer the question.'

'I can't. I don't know.' She could feel her irritation with Balinski growing. 'It's not something I ever discussed with her. I mean, why would I? She was a fit, healthy woman in her late fifties or early sixties. I don't even know how old she was, let alone who benefits from her death. She was my boss! In fact, as far as I can see, no one benefits from her death, at least, no one who works at Phoenix Publishing.'

'I'll get someone on to it. Now, any idea where this Marius person might be hanging out?'

'He wasn't at Alwyn Hall when I left this morning. Well, his car wasn't in the parking area. I've no idea where he'd go.'

'And you believe he's not likely to find where his nieces are hiding out?'

'That was the whole point. Marius doesn't know about my uncle's house, so he won't able to find them.'

'OK, I'm going to make a few calls. Wait here.' Balinski left the room, and Sam finished her now cold cup of tea.

'How's it going, guv?' asked DC Chaudhury. 'You've had a call from an Inspector Bevan, from the Gwent force. He wants you to call him. Said it was urgent.'

'Right, I'll call him now, and I'll fill you in later. Sam Holliday's in the interview room. I'll talk to her again when I've made the call. Have you spoken to Jen Somerville?'

'Yes. I need to fill you in on that to see if it ties in with the story you've got from Sam.'

Balinski nodded and went in to a side office to make the call, frustrating DC Chaudhury who was unable to hear a word of what was said.

'I see,' said Balinski, tapping his fingers on the desk. 'Well, that ties in with what I've heard from Sam Holliday. They've either rehearsed their stories very carefully, or they're telling the truth.' He paused, listening to Bevan's reply. 'I agree, I don't see why they'd fabricate something so complicated, especially one where the Morgans are implicated.' He listened for a few minutes as Bevan explained what he was going to do next.

'OK, I'll finish talking to Sam Holliday and get a formal statement from her. Let me know how you proceed with the Morgans and the other two. What about the nieces?'

Bevan explained his current thinking. 'OK. No, I won't mention any of this to the two women here. Yes, yes, speak soon. Thanks for updating me. Goodbye.' Balinski ended the call, frowning. *Why did another police force always have to get involved? It'll be just like the last case when Keld took all the credit.* Balinski pushed his chair back from the table, using so much force it tipped over. He righted it, and went out to finish his interview with Sam.

'All right, guv?' asked DC Chaudhury. 'I heard a bit of a clatter.'

'Fine,' muttered Balinski. A quick glance at his grim expression made her immediately turn back to her computer screen.

'I'm coming to London. Then we go to this place in Wales and sort everything out. We'll find your nieces. And we will grow more cannabis.' Marius winced as his boss, Constantin, shouted down the phone.

'OK. You'll come here, and I can drive you to Alwyn Hall,' said Marius.

'Yes, yes, whatever,' agreed Constantin. 'Is there anything about that woman on the news?'

'Someone's identified the body. She was the woman who owned the publishing company. She's dead, and that book dies with her. Good riddance,' said Marius.

'The police have not linked her with you—or the cannabis?'

'No. The news said the death was being treated as suspicious, but there was nothing about trying to find who killed her. Or anything else. Anyway, I didn't kill her. It was just a tap on her head.'

'Hmm,' said Constantin. 'Perhaps your 'tap' was stronger than you realised. But I don't care. If the cannabis is safe, that's all I care about.'

'And what about Cristina and Elena,' said Marius.

'They are your problem. You brought them here. You find them and get them back to Romania.'

There was a pause while Marius absorbed what Constantin had said. 'When will you get to London?' asked Marius.

'Tonight. Then we go to Wales.'

Morgan took his pouch of tobacco off the shelf of the dresser with shaking hands. 'God, what a day,' he said, falling into a chair. He looked across at Carys, who was grey with tiredness.

'It feels even worse than before we went to the police,' she said. 'I don't want to go to prison. I can't cope with all this. And we'll have to cancel the schools that were coming next week. What are we going to do?'

'First off, make some tea. Isn't that what everyone does in a crisis?' Morgan asked.

Carys got up to put the kettle on, the familiarity of the task calming her slightly. 'Will you call the schools in the morning?'

'OK. I'll have to think of something. Perhaps … a problem with the roof. Yes, that's a good one.'

'Whatever you think. I don't know whether to wish Marius comes back or not.'

'It'll push everything to a head if he does. You know what the

Inspector said, we're to contact him as soon as Marius gets here. Oh—talk of the devil,' he said, as his phone started to ring.

'Hello. Everything all right?' asked Morgan. 'Right you are. I'll make up another room then. See you tomorrow morning.'

'That was the man himself,' said Morgan. 'He's coming back early tomorrow, with his boss, apparently. We'll need to sort out a room for him in the tower.'

'Dear God,' said Carys, 'as if I haven't got enough on my plate without another uninvited guest! OK, OK, I'll do it.'

'I'll call Bevan. You know what this will mean?' said Morgan. 'And I'd better let Aidan and Nate know.'

'There'll be a police raid then.' She looked at Morgan, the fear all too apparent. 'Well, good,' she said. 'I hope Marius gets his comeuppance, whatever it means for us. I'll be in the tower if you need me for anything.'

Sam checked her phone for the umpteenth time that morning. She'd spoken to Nate after he and Aidan had talked to the police, and she had told him that she had identified Charlotte.

'God, I'm so sorry, Sam. That's such an upsetting thing to have to do. I wish I could have been with you,' said Nate.

'I wish you were here too, but at least I had Jen. And the mortuary staff were really kind. Balinski wasn't too bad either. I remembered Charlotte told me she was going to get the CCTV set up but apparently the server was at the heart of the fire so everything would have been destroyed. He was a bit incredulous about the whole story at first but by the time he'd finished interviewing me, he got a call from Inspector Bevan who'd heard the same story from you and Aidan. How did it go with Bevan?'

'All right. He seems a reasonable sort. He didn't seem too pleased to see us at first, but when he heard what we wanted to tell him—well, he was all ears. I don't think Morgan or Carys knew what had hit them. We've all been told to stay at Alwyn Hall for now. The police won't act immediately, but if Marius returns then they'll be a raid, for sure. He's too big a fish to get away.'

'Are you and Aidan definitely all right? It must have been exhausting. I know how the police like to go over every detail,' said Sam.

'We're fine. Just shattered. I'm not sure when we'll be able to come home—soon, I hope. That room was bad enough when you were with me, but now it's just Gustav and me it's a bit grim.'

'It can't be for long. You haven't done anything wrong, so the police have got no reason to keep you. But you know all that, as an ex-police officer.' said Sam.

'Yes, I know it, but I was on the investigating side before, not the witness or potential suspect side like I am now. They've only got my word and Aidan's that we're not involved.'

Sam took a deep breath. She hadn't thought of that. 'But they'll soon find you're not part of it, won't they?'

'Yep, it might just take a bit of time. To be fair, I think they want us to stay at Alwyn Hall so they know where we are, and that it looks a bit more normal if Marius does come back. Don't worry about us.'

'What about Morgan and Carys?'

'Oh, Morgan and Carys. Well, I think it's just starting to sink in that this is the end of the road. They're going to cancel next week's school bookings. They will be arrested, but what happens from there, I'm not sure. Anyway, I'm going to grab some food, and settle in for the night. What about you?'

'Much the same. It's been a long day, with the drive as well.'

'I'll call you in the morning. Take care,' said Nate, the tenderness in his voice making the simple words more meaningful.

'You too. I ..., well, give Gustav a pat from me.' She'd nearly said she loved him. *Why didn't I* she thought. But that was too big a question for this evening.

Nate messaged her early next morning to say Morgan had told him that Marius was expected back that morning, but she'd heard nothing since. Sam could not stay in the house any longer. The wait to find out what was happening at Alwyn Hall was unbearable. And she wanted—or rather, she *didn't* want—to see the damage to Phoenix's offices for herself. She had no idea if other staff had been officially notified that the office would be closed for the foreseeable. As it was a holiday weekend, it may be the first people knew about it was when they tried to go in to work.

She set off, her phone in her pocket, still on edge as she waited for Nate's call. She hurried through the quiet streets of Lower Rushford, oblivious today of the beauty of the town that she usually took time to admire.

As she turned the corner, she saw the police tape that blocked off entry to the building. A police officer was outside, looking bored.

'Good morning. I'm Sam Holliday. I work here.'

'Not today … and not for quite a few days, I'd say,' said the policeman.

'I know … I know what happened here. DS Balinski told me. Do you know if staff have been notified?'

'No idea. Presumably whoever runs this place will do that.'

'That's the problem. Charlotte McManners—the Chief Executive—was the person who died here.'

'Ah, I see. Well, not much we can do about that.'

Sam looked at him with some frustration.

'I'll call DS Balinski and ask him then,' said Sam.

'Right you are.'

Sam looked up at the building. It didn't look too bad from the outside, but inside was likely going to be a mess. With a heavy heart, she turned away, and walked around the corner to make the call.

'The whole computer system will be down,' said Balinski, 'so you won't be able to get staff details that way. Were there HR files—I mean old-fashioned paper files?'

'Possibly. Could I go in and check—with a police officer, of course?' Sam asked.

'I'll see what I can sort out. I'll give you a call back.'

It only took a few minutes. Her phone buzzed and her heart leaped: Nate! But of course it was Balinski.

'The policeman you spoke to outside the building will escort you in. Follow his instructions to the letter, and do not touch anything unnecessarily. Be as quick as you can,' he said.

Sam returned to the office. The policeman had clearly been briefed.

'The outside stairs will be easier. The revolving door isn't working,' the policeman said. She climbed the stairs slowly, remembering how scared she'd been of the open ironwork the first time she'd had to use these stairs. She resisted the temptation to look down and very soon she reached the door to the second floor. The policeman opened it, and they went inside.

On this floor, everything looked as it always did. A quick glance at the first floor looked undamaged too. As she reached the bottom of the stairs and entered the ground floor, the full extent of the damage hit her. Scorch marks stained the walls, chairs and desks showed burn marks or had melted corners, and the server cupboard was completely destroyed. Her hand over her mouth and nose in an ineffective attempt to block the smell, she looked around in dismay: dismay not only for the devastation, but for the realisation that she was close to where Charlotte had died.

'All right, there?' asked the policeman. 'Don't go any further. It's a crime scene, remember.'

'No, no, I won't. I need to find the HR files.' With legs wobbling, Sam made her way to the office of the woman who looked after HR and general admin work. She felt uncomfortable looking through the files, noting the details of a few key people who could probably notify other colleagues.

'OK, that's all I need, thank you.'

It was a relief to leave the office behind her. Walking through town, she had a sudden yearning for coffee, and as Gino's, the Italian café was open, she went in. She was greeted as an old friend, and of course the first question was about what was happening at Phoenix.

'We heard the news about your boss. This is terrible! I am so sorry. Coffee is on the house—I insist!' said Gino, looking upset.

'Thank you, Gino, that's very kind. One of your cappuccinos would be wonderful.'

The café was quiet, and Sam settled into a corner seat. She checked her phone. No call from Nate, and no message. She hoped everything was going well … is that what she meant? It was unlikely to go well for everyone at Alwyn Hall, but all she wanted was for Nate and Aidan to come home, with Gustav, of course. And the girls! She's almost forgotten about them. She'd have to talk to Nate about them.

She smiled at Gino as he placed her cappuccino carefully on the table, with a couple of amaretti biscuits nestling in the saucer.

'You're a life saver, Gino, thank you.'

As she sipped her coffee she started to think how she would explain what had happened to her colleagues. The more she thought about it, the more she realised how much she could *not* tell them—for now, at least. They knew about the anonymous letters. But they didn't know about Alwyn Hall, or why Morgan was so desperate to separate Alwyn Hall from the book. And she certainly couldn't tell them about Marius and the link with Romania. She sighed. All she could say that it was definitely Charlotte who had died, and that the offices were currently closed. They could work from home, but it wasn't yet clear how Phoenix would operate—if it could continue at all. While everyone had work to do, how would they be paid?

She checked her phone again. Nothing. Her coffee finished, she smiled her goodbye at Gino who was now serving other customers, and walked home.

Settling herself at her breakfast bar, she got out her notebook and phone. The obvious person to call first was Jen, who picked up after a couple of rings.

'What's happening? Have you heard?' asked Jen, her anxiety obvious.

'Nothing after Nate's message about Marius. I imagine the place is swarming with police. Nate's expecting he and Aidan will need to convince the police they're not involved in the cannabis business, so it may take a while before they're free to leave.'

'Jumping jellybeans!' said Jen. 'I hadn't thought of that.'

'Try not to worry. I know it's easier said than done. Now, changing the subject, I've just gone into the office.'

'What's it like?' asked Jen.

'A bit of a mess, to say the least, but the first and second floors are OK. So once we can get back in the building, people can work on those floors. I'm just not sure whether Phoenix can carry on without Charlotte. Anyway, I think we need to get in touch with colleagues. That's why I went into the office, to get some contact details. I thought you could help me with that? I know you're freelance now, but you know nearly everyone.'

'Of course I will. Shall I come over to your place?'

'That would be great. I'll make a start. We're going to have to be careful what we tell people,' warned Sam.

Sam ended her last call. 'I don't want to do anything like this again,' she said. 'Is it too early for a glass of wine?'

'It's … nearly 4. And it has been a really tough day,' said Jen.

'I'm convinced,' said Sam, reaching for the glasses and taking a bottle out of the fridge. She had just poured the first glass when her phone rang. 'It's Nate—at last! Hi, hi, how are you? Are you OK? What about Aidan? Gustav?' Jen gave her a quizzical look as Sam chuckled. Sam gave her a quick thumbs up.

'Oh, good old Gustav! What a hero! So Morgan and Carys are under arrest? And Marius and his friend?' There was a pause as she listened intently to Nate. 'That is awful. What a horrible pair they are. Poor Elena and Cristina. Oh, and what's happening about them?' Again, Sam listened, and Jen fidgeted, sipping her wine.

'What about you and Aidan? Can you come home?' The answer was clearly 'yes' as Sam's face lit up. 'I can't wait. Jen's here—and she's grinning from ear to ear. We'll both be glad when you and Aidan are out of that place. OK, that makes sense. So, we'll expect you sometime tomorrow afternoon then? Brilliant, can't wait. Say hi to Aidan for me, and a big pat for Gustav. We're so glad you're all

OK and those thugs can't do any more harm. Take care, see you tomorrow.'

'Tell me everything,' begged Jen. 'It sounds as though everyone's getting their just deserts.'

'Definitely, but wait until you hear about Marius and his boss, Constantin,' said Sam. 'But first, wine. Tell you what, I'll fill you in and then shall we order a takeaway? I'm famished, and I can't be bothered with cooking. I don't think I've got anything in anyway. Nate said he and Aidan have booked into the pub for tonight. They can't stay at Alwyn Hall now and they don't want to drive home this evening so they'll drive here tomorrow morning.'

'Makes sense—and I'm with you on the takeaway,' said Jen, as she and Sam picked up their glasses and headed to the comfy chair and sofa. 'Right, I'm all ears …'

Sam looked around the table at Nate, Aidan and Jen. 'Don't let it get cold. Tuck in!' she said.

'Mmm, smells wonderful,' said Jen. Sam had shopped in the morning. She felt Nate, Aidan, and Gustav's homecoming deserved celebrating. She'd kept it simple: a favourite chicken and tarragon dish, with new potatoes and vegetables, with a crumble for pudding. Comfort food: they needed comfort as well as celebration.

'I'll pour the wine, shall I?' said Nate. 'None of us are driving anywhere this evening,' he said, as he poured generous glasses for them all. Nate was staying at Sam's, and Aidan was going to sleep on the sofa at Jen's. Nate looked across at Sam, a small frown furrowing her brow.

'How about we raise our glasses in memory of Charlotte. Do you want to say a few words, Sam?' asked Nate.

'That's a nice idea. I keep thinking about her. She was a lovely person, and she was doing a great job with Phoenix. I just wish I had known her for longer.' Jen and Aidan nodded their agreement. 'So … to Charlotte, and all that she did for Phoenix.' The four clicked glasses, and savoured their wine, sombre for a couple of minutes.

Breaking the quietness, Jen asked Nate to tell them what had happened after she and Sam left Alwyn Hall. 'Sam told me the story, but I'd really like to hear it from you and Aidan. That is, if you don't mind.'

'No, I don't mind,' said Nate. 'I'm just relieved to have got away from there, and that the police didn't want to question us further. We both had to make a statement but that was all straightforward.'

'Did you see any of the action?' asked Jen.

'Some of it. As soon as Morgan told Bevan that Marius was coming back to Alwyn Hall and bringing his boss with him, things must have really moved fast back at the police station. We tried to keep out of the way at the Hall, but we heard Marius and his boss arrive early yesterday morning. They went off to the tower, where their rooms were. Then Morgan knocked on my door. He looked furious, and scared. Apparently, Marius's boss was the same boss that Morgan had supposedly killed in the car crash in Romania! Constantin and Morgan had orchestrated it to put Morgan in a position where he'd agree to growing the cannabis. They'd assumed Morgan wouldn't recognise him from the accident as Morgan was in shock, and it was dark. But he remembered seeing the scar and Morgan recognised him from that.'

'What?' said Sam and Jen together. 'You didn't tell me that on the phone,' Sam added.

'Sorry. It was all such chaos. Poor old Morgan, he does have the most appalling luck. I told you about Gustav, didn't I?' said Nate.

'You did, but tell us again. He was such a hero!' said Sam.

'Well, at one point, Marius and Constantin tried to make a run for it. The armed police shouted a warning for them to stop. Gustav didn't like Marius—remember how he growled at him when we first met him?' The others nodded. 'Suddenly, Gustav broke free of his lead—I was holding on to him but not firmly enough, as it happened. I've never seen Gustav move so fast. He was a streak of lightning, and he grabbed Marius's trouser leg and brought him down. Constantin hesitated, which was his undoing, because it gave one of the policemen a chance to rugby-tackle him. They were both soon in handcuffs, and heading off to the police station.'

Gustav, who was settled on a rug lifted his head when he heard the name 'Marius' and growled quietly.

'It's OK, Gustav, we won't be seeing him again, or his boss,' said Nate.

'You were brilliant, Gustav,' said Jen. Gustav gave a snuffled woof and lowered his head back down to continue dozing.

'Did you see Morgan and Carys?' Jen asked Nate and Aidan.

'Only when they were both getting into police cars. We didn't get a chance to talk to them once the police arrived. Everything happened so quickly,' said Nate.

'Let's hope those Romanians get their comeuppance,' said Aidan. There were murmurs of agreement from around the table.

'What about Elena and Cristina?' asked Sam.

'I explained about them to the police. We weren't allowed to go to the house, as the police wanted to talk to them. I assume they'll have to make statements, and they may be arrested even though they were coerced into working for Marius for all that time. But they were couriering cannabis, albeit against their will. I really don't know what will happen,' said Nate.

'I feel a bit bad about them,' said Sam. 'I tried to keep them safe … but I suppose they knew at some point they'd have to face the music. There's no way they could just travel back to Romania after staying here so long.'

'I know. Well, maybe either Bevan or Balinski will give us an update at some point. Now, let's talk about other things. What's the chances of Aidan's book being published now?' said Nate.

'I really don't know,' said Sam. 'We'll have to wait and see who's going to take over Phoenix. For now, we're all at a loose end. It's a weird situation to be in.'

'Let's hope something gets sorted out soon,' said Aidan.

August 2024

Sam brought the last of the dishes to the table. It had been three months since Nate, Aidan, Jen and Sam had had an opportunity to get together for a meal. She hadn't been sure what to cook for them, but as the smell of spices filled the air, she knew she'd made the right choice.

'This smells so good,' said Aidan, lifting the lid off one of the dishes. 'Mmm, I can smell cinnamon.'

'I hope there's something here you'll all like,' said Sam.

'I can't believe you cooked it all,' said Jen, looking impressed. 'I can't wait to try it all.'

'Before we dig in, I think we should have a toast: to *Superswamp* and everyone who made publication possible!' said Sam.

'Too many to name,' said Aidan, 'but a huge thank you from me to all of you. The book wouldn't be here without any of you.'

'Let's have another look at it,' said Jen. 'There aren't many books that have had to get through as many hoops as this one. I know getting published is tough, but for *Superswamp* it was super tough!'

The others laughed. Aidan held up his copy of *Superswamp*, smiling broadly. 'I wasn't sure I'd ever see it in print,' he said. 'But it is—and that's thanks to the new MD of Phoenix. The next toast has to be … to Sam, Phoenix's MD!'

Looking a little embarrassed at the attention, Sam clinked her glass with the others. 'I still can't take it in, really,' she said. 'When Charlotte's lawyers called me into their offices, I had no idea what I was going to hear. When they told me she'd bequeathed Phoenix to me, plus enough money to invest in its future, I thought I was dreaming.'

'A good dream, and not a nightmare?' asked Jen.

'Definitely not a nightmare. I did ask myself if I really could do it. But the alternative, to let Phoenix go and everyone's jobs with it, was something I couldn't let happen. So here I am: a rookie MD, with twenty employees … and a new book out! Hopefully it'll still make good Christmas sales—there's been enough publicity for it!'

'There has. I had no idea I'd be in so much demand for interviews,' said Aidan.

'Nor me,' said Jen. 'Jumping jellybeans, what a turn up for the books.'

'I couldn't have put it better,' said Sam, laughing.

'Any news of Morgan, or Carys and the girls?' asked Jen. 'Sorry to ask, but I have been thinking about them.'

'Yes, Morgan and Carys will have to appear in court. Apparently, given the circumstances and that they turned themselves in—and helped the police to arrest Marius and Constantin—they're likely to get a suspended sentence,' said Aidan.

'Good. Well, it's not good, but at least there's a chance they won't end up in prison,' said Jen. 'I don't think they've deserved that.'

'I liked Carys. She was trying to support Morgan, and she tried to look out for Elena and Cristina,' said Sam.

'What about the girls?' asked Jen.

'I got a message a couple of weeks ago,' Aidan continued. 'They're back in Romania, but not at home. They've found themselves somewhere to live in Bucharest and they're giving English lessons to pay their way. Their time in the UK meant their English improved—although I think their students will learn to speak with a hint of a Welsh accent!'

'That's funny,' said Jen. 'Well, sort of funny. I don't suppose they feel they can go home, after everything that happened.'

'No. I don't think they wanted to go back to the family home. I don't think their family really understands why they disappeared for so long, or how Marius ended up being arrested and deported,' said Aidan.

'Hopefully he and Constantin are rotting together in some unsavoury Romanian jail,' said Jen with surprising vehemence.

'Jen, that's not like you!' said Sam.

Gustav pushed his head into Jen's lap. 'I'm with Gustav,' she said. 'I'd have bitten their ankles, given half a chance!' Everyone laughed, and even Gustav looked as though he was grinning.

'To Phoenix, and all the books to follow,' said Nate, smiling at Sam. Once again, the four raised their glasses, before turning their attention to the feast Sam had prepared for them.

'Oh, that would be wonderful. Lots of lovely books—and no more murders!' said Sam.

With Thanks

As always, I've greatly appreciated the encouragement and support of friends and family who make time to read my drafts and give me feedback. It's a much better book for your input! In particular, I'd like to thank Linda Gray, Sue Rudge, Caroline Phillips, Mark McArthur-Christie, and Pippa Shay. Also my grand-daughter, Niamh Palmer, who gave very helpful feedback on the scenes about the school residential trip.

And of course: Jon Franklin, thank you for all your support and encouragement, and for the many cups of coffee (made using a Moka pot, of course!).

Printed in Dunstable, United Kingdom

77256606R00111